'If you devoured *The Hunger* (

The Ti

'Taut and suspense packed right up to the last page.'
The Financial Times

'A fast-paced thriller in which nothing is as it seems.'
The Independent

'A beautifully crafted complex thriller.'
The Independent on Sunday

'A gripping story, impossible to put down.
Green cranks up the tension with every page.'
L. A. Weatherly,
bestselling author of *Angel*

'Had me holding my breath every
nail-biting step of the way.'
Chicklish

Recommended by Radio 4 Open Book

Caroline Green is an experienced freelance journalist who has written stories since she was a little girl. She vividly remembers a family walk when she was ten years old when she was so preoccupied with thoughts of her new 'series' that she almost walked into a tree.

Caroline lives in North London with her husband, two sporty sons and one very bouncy labrador retriever.

Her first novel, *Dark Ride*, was longlisted for the Branford Boase award and won the RNA Young Adult award.

Praise for *Dark Ride*:

'Full of tension, mystery and real-life drama, Dark Ride is not to be missed.' Chicklish

'Almost impossible to put down.' Goodreads

'Fresh and convincing.' Booktrust

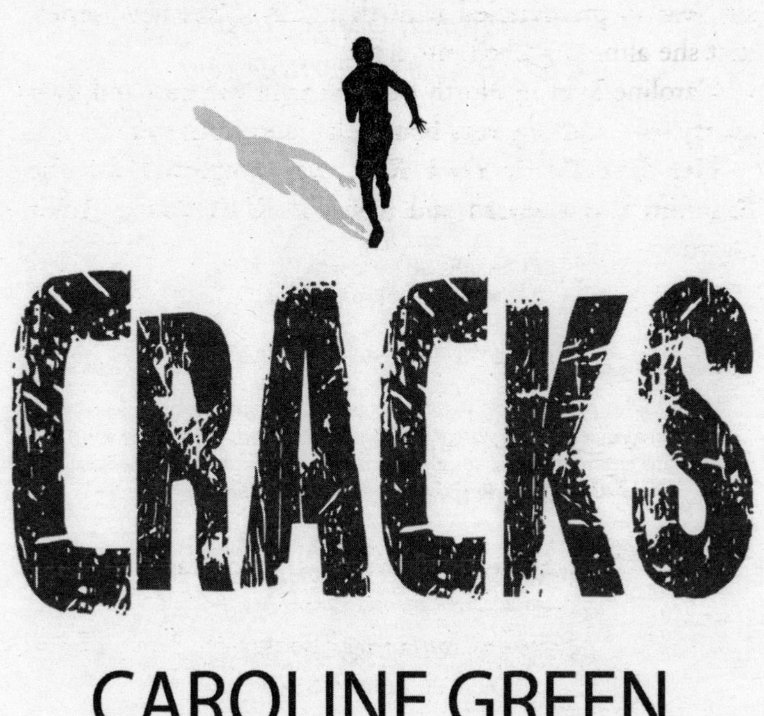

CAROLINE GREEN

PICCADILLY PRESS • LONDON

For my dad, George Green,
who gave me the writing gene

First published in Great Britain in 2012
by Piccadilly Press Ltd,
5 Castle Road, London NW1 8PR
www.piccadillypress.co.uk

A catalogue record for this book is available
from the British Library

ISBN: 978 1 84812 168 3 (paperback)

Also available as an ebook

3 5 7 9 10 8 6 4 2

Printed in Great Britain by CPI Group (UK), Croydon, CR0 4YY
Cover design by Simon Davis

PART I

CHAPTER 1

eggs

The first crack is freaky.

I'm alone in the boys' toilets at the end of break-time. Everyone else has drifted off to class. I'm just washing my hands when there's a creaking, groaning sound like a dying cow above me. I look up to see a dirty great crack racing across the ceiling. A piece of plaster falls off and just misses my head. I run out, straight into my maths teacher.

Peters says, 'Why aren't you in your classroom? Didn't you hear the —'

'The roof's coming down, sir!'

'What? Show me.'

He goes in first. 'What are you talking about? I can't see anything.'

I follow him in.

The ceiling looks exactly as it always does. There are no

cracks. Toilet paper glue-balls cover it like constellations of grotty stars.

'Is this some kind of joke?' sighs Peters. 'You'd better get yourself along to your lesson,' he says. 'Think yourself lucky I'm not giving you detention.'

He walks off down the corridor.

I take one last quick look up and then get out of there as fast as I can.

The second crack is even freakier.

You have to climb a huge hill to get to our bungalow. It sits right on the top, like the massive zit my stepdad once had on his bald head. I made the mistake of laughing and he slapped me round the face so hard my teeth played tunes.

His name is Desmond, Des for short, and he has a son called Pigface. Of course, he isn't really called Pigface. He's called Ryan, but he has a face like a pig and is half as smart.

Des must know Pigface is an idiot, but you'd better not criticise him. I guess that's why they say blood's thicker than water. My mum, Tina, is all right, but she has a huge blind spot when it comes to Des. She says things like, 'I deserve a bit of happiness, Cal, don't spoil it for me. Can't you all just try to get on with each other?' Deep down in a place I don't visit too often, I reckon there's something a bit missing with her maternal affections, to be honest.

As I was saying, we live – Pigface, Desmondo, Mum and me – in a bungalow at the top of the hill. If you manage to get there without coughing up one of your lungs, you can stop for a minute and take in the lovely view.

There's the brewery on the edge of town. It has a permanent cloud coming out of the giant chimney, like in a kid's drawing. Except this one isn't fluffy and white, it's black and filled with chemicals and muck. There's school, in case I try to forget about it between three-thirty p.m. and eight-thirty a.m. And there's the top of Riley Hall, the young offenders' place where they put all the bad lads. As in, 'If you don't do your homework/eat your peas/stop picking your nose you'll end up in Riley.' I sometimes imagine Pigface getting locked up in there for some crime he's bound to commit (I'm thinking something involving violence is most likely) and then Des topping himself in his grief.

I can dream, can't I?

I haven't been first back to the bungalow for ages because I've been going running every night or doing circuit training at school. I go to the hiding place to get the key, which is under the car that sits on bricks at the front of the house. FYI, there's also an old sink and a toilet from when Des started to do our bathroom. Over there is the shed, or, as I still think of it, **The Shed**. Des used to shove me in there to teach me a lesson sometimes and it was filled with spiders and webs and general horror. There are loads of old petrol cans too from when Des had a phase of doing up cars. The whole thing could have gone *boom* with the slightest spark. Des's massive thighs rubbing together in their polyester trackie bottoms would be enough to do it. Now though, it's where he keeps the proceeds from his other 'business'. It's got a load of old fertiliser, packs of foreign batteries and a load of alarm clocks that don't work, among other tat.

We don't even bother hiding the key to the house that well. It's not like we have much to nick inside, although Pigface has his beloved Xbox, which he never lets me near. Not that this stops me from playing on it all the time when he's not there. If I'm not playing on it, I'm pretty much thinking about when I'll get my next chance. I wander into his room, intending to have a go on *Call of Duty*. First, I pick up one of his weights and give it an experimental lift. Not too bad. I must be getting stronger even though I still need to use both hands. I lift it higher and wave it about a bit, dancing on my toes.

'Look at me, Pigface!' I say. 'Think you're so tough, yeah? Yeah? One day I'm going to kick your fat —'

I don't mean to let go of the weight, really I don't. But it slips out of my hand. And lands right on top of the Xbox with a sickening crunch. The room shrinks around me and my vision goes all blurry. I think I'm going to be sick . . . Then I spring into action, frantically trying to turn it on. But it's dead.

I've gone and killed Pigface's Xbox!

'Oh God, oh God, oh God, oh God . . .' I'm gibbering as I look pointlessly around the room for a magic device that will turn back time and make it not have happened. I can't stand to look at it, all broken and accusing, so I run into the

living room, heart pounding and mouth dry, trying to think.

I hear a noise outside and the shock feels like someone has unzipped my skin. I flick back the grey lace curtain and peer out. But there's no one there.

I'm standing in the middle of the room, quivering all over when there's this beeping sound. It starts quietly and then gets louder and louder so I have to cover my ears. I feel like my head will pop like a balloon.

Then a voice says the word, *'Stabilising,'* so close to me I wheel round and shout 'Who's there?' but there's no one. Something makes me glance down at my hands and I see they're covered in hundreds of tiny spots. But they're not really spots, they're lights. Like someone's pointing hundreds of lasers at me. I try to shake them away and they switch right off and everything is normal again. I look out the window but all I can see is a small black and white cat, which seems familiar, and is staring at me in that sod-you cat way.

Cracks in the ceiling . . . weird voices . . . funny lights. Maybe it's my mind that's going.

I'm so freaked out that my teeth clack like falsies and I collapse on the sofa. I'm still sitting there, thinking hard about not thinking, when Des walks into the room, holding a bag of groceries.

'What's the matter with you?' he says.

'Nothing, just chillaxin,' I say, really unconvincingly.

Des stares at me like he's never seen anything so pointless. 'Well, you can get off your arse and put this shopping away.'

I follow him into the kitchen. You don't argue with Des. He weighs about seventeen stone and looks like he's carrying triplets in that belly. He's bald, like I said, and his head and neck are about the same width. It's as though he has one big fat column of flesh with facial features at the top. He smokes and likes his fry-ups and lager. Really, he's a heart attack waiting to happen. Sometimes I slip him some of my chips just to speed things up a bit.

I put the milk and cheese into the fridge and Des sparks up a fag. They all smoke in this house. If we had a guinea pig, it'd be on the B&H too, I swear.

I cough, even though I don't really need to.

'Oh, I'm sorry, is my evil cigarette bothering you, Princess?' says Des.

He often calls me 'princess'. That's the kind of comic genius he is.

I ignore him and start to put the bread away. He walks up to me, smiles, and blows a big gust of smoke right into my face, so close I can smell his eggie lunch. I cough for real then and he laughs as he leaves the room.

My eyes are streaming and I wipe my face, picturing Des driving off a cliff to make myself feel better. Then I do a dumb squeak and shoot back about three metres because . . .

. . . there's a massive crack right down the middle of the kitchen table.

It makes a groaning sound as one side keels over, and a box of eggs crashes to the ground.

I almost shout for Des but, remembering what happened

in the bogs, I force myself to stop. I close my eyes and open them again and, in that instant, everything is back as it was before. Except for the eggs, which are lying on the floor in a smushed mess.

Just at that moment, Des strolls back into the room. 'You useless little sod – did you drop those?'

No, Des, I'm suddenly seeing giant cracks appearing everywhere. And by the way, I've knackered your son's Xbox.

'Sorry.'

'Well, you're paying for them,' says Des, filling the kettle with water. 'Eggs don't grow on trees.'

'Don't they?'

I really need to learn to keep my gob shut. For a fat bloke, he can move surprisingly fast. He's across the room and holding my chin in his meaty fist in a split second. His piggy eyes narrow so much they almost disappear. He's so close I can hear the wheeze in his breathing and see all the beardy dots on his chin.

'Now, you know that I love Tina to pieces, don't you?' he says in a dangerously quiet voice.

I nod, or try to. He's gripping me so hard my bottom lip is folded in half.

'But you . . . you're nothing to me. Nothing. You're nobody. Do you understand? Nobody.'

I nod. He's really hurting me now.

'And if you think you can cheek me, you're going to find your backside kicked into the end of next week. Now clean those eggs and get out of my sight.' He lets go and carries on making his brew.

I get the dustpan and start to sweep up the broken eggs, darting glances at the table to check it's still in one piece.

It's been a very weird day.

Chapter 2

hit me

Des goes off to collect Mum and Pigface from work and I hurry back into Pigface's room. I pull out cables and put them back in again, giving the telly a thump, just in case. But it's no use. This Xbox is a goner.

Some old song comes into my head . . . something about it being the end of the world and feeling fine.

It's the end of the world all right, but I definitely don't feel fine. My heart keeps pounding and my vision's funny. It's like I'm looking through a weird lens. The edges of everything feel blurred, distorted. Like none of it's real. When I come out of the room a few minutes later and hear the sound of the car, my stomach twists and my heart races even faster. Maybe I could just slip out the back door and never come back?

'. . . now make sure you leave those boots outside, Ryan, they're filthy.'

'Yeah, yeah, keep your hair on,' says Pigface and I hear Des laugh.

Mum comes through the door, frowning. Des lets Pigface say what he likes to Mum.

'Stick the kettle on,' she says by way of hello and flops into a chair to take off her shoes. She flexes her toes and then bends over to rub them, groaning a bit. Des comes in next, smiling at something his darling boy has said and his smile slides right off his face when he sees me.

'What are you staring at?' he says.

I turn away. 'Nothing.' I put the kettle on. Mum's talking about something that happened in the supermarket where she works but I can't really concentrate. I hear the unmistakable sound of Pigface lumbering into the kitchen and keep my back turned to him.

'I'll have a coffee,' he says, 'and make sure you put a decent spoonful in it this time. Last one you made was like gnat's pee.'

Normally, I would say something like, 'Make your own,' or 'What did your last slave die from?' but today I just dip my head and spoon coffee into cups.

There's a change in the air like a drop in pressure. I realise there's no hope of him not finding out what I've done. He may be thick but he's got these super-senses, like an animal. I can feel his eyes boring into me but I ignore him as I put the coffees onto the kitchen table. I almost hear the heavy clanking of his brain working as he wonders why I'm being such a good little slave.

'Ooh, I need this,' says Mum, fishing for her fags in the

pocket of her blue checked overall and closing her eyes as she lights one.

Des is talking to someone on his mobile phone but picks up the coffee and slurps loudly anyway. He runs a business putting bathrooms in but he's obviously rubbish at it because he's always getting customers ringing up and yelling at him.

'Yeah, well, I may have said Wednesday but I never said it would be *this* Wednesday, did I?' he says, walking out of the room.

Pigface is still watching me. I look away but may as well have a neon sign saying, *I've messed with your stuff* above my head. He pushes past me to go to his room and I get a strong whiff of his pits.

I'm thinking about whether I can run when I hear Pigface swear at the top of his voice and I know he's found the broken Xbox and worked out who did it. He may be big, but I'm fast. I'm out of my chair and heading for the back door before he comes steaming into the room. Mum says, 'What's going —?' but I don't hear the rest because Pigface is screaming, really screaming what he's going to do to me.

I race round to the front of the house, thinking I'll have to run away, anywhere . . . and I smack straight into Des's wobbly belly. He grabs my shoulders and shakes me, hard.

'What do you think you're doing?' he spits.

'Let me go! He's gonna kill me!'

I wrench away from his grip but then Pigface is there, his eyes almost bulging out of his head and bits of spit flying through the air. Time seems to slow down and for a moment, it's the weirdest thing, but I can see the whole scene like I'm watching it on widescreen. Each drop of Pigface's spit is suspended in the air like tiny jewels. The front door's open and Mum is a silhouette in a puddle of warm light, watching and slowly smoking a fag like she's watching all this on telly.

Pigface pulls his fist back, his face twisted with hate. I close my eyes instinctively, bracing myself. And then nothing happens. I open one eye. Pigface's meaty fist is about a centimetre from my face. It's vibrating slightly and he can't seem to move it. His face is a picture. It's like there's a forcefield between us or someone's holding him back. And then there's a whoosh and everything comes back to full speed. Des and Mum are both shouting but it's not clear at who. Pigface storms back into the house.

I start laughing. I can't help it.

'Did you see that?' I say.

'You think everything's a joke, do you?' snarls Des. 'Well, next time I'm not holding him back.'

Like he was! He was standing miles away, watching.

'Yeah, but did you see what —?'

'Shut up, Cal,' snaps Mum. 'I can't believe you think this is funny. You don't help yourself, you really don't.'

'No, but —'

'SHUT IT!' Des slams his fist into the other hand and even Mum flinches. He continues in a low growl. 'Get to your room and don't come out.'

I look at Mum but she's avoiding my eye so I slink off to

my bedroom and flump onto the bed, face down. Eventually I take off my clothes and crawl into the bed even though it's still early.

My thoughts are going round and round in my head. The cracks in the boys' bogs and the smashing eggs were enough to cope with. Pigface's mysterious floating fist is even weirder still. What's happening to me? Am I going mad?

I'm certain I don't fall asleep, really certain. So I can't explain why the next thing I know it's morning and I'm in the bathroom in my school uniform brushing my teeth. It's like someone jumped a scene ahead on a DVD.

Nobody says very much at breakfast. Pigface acts like I'm not even there. I wonder whether he's a bit scared of me and this gave me such a buzz I almost laugh out loud. Des is stomping around with a bit of toast in one hand and a cig hanging out the side of his mouth. He's speaking into his phone and saying something about 'problems with the suppliers'.

It feels like there's no air in the house so I'm glad when it's time to walk to school. The sun is shining and the birds are tweeting away. It's a bit hard to stress about mystery cracks and the general horror that is my life this morning.

I knock for Amil, who lives on the road behind the school.

Even though he's my best friend, he doesn't come to the house. The one time he did, Des took one look at him and could barely bring himself to speak. I reckoned it might have something to do with Amil's brown skin and I burned with shame.

I'm always at his, though. I love it there. He lives above the newsagent's on the high street, which his parents own. There are always loads of people crammed into the tiny, hot living room upstairs when the shop's closed. His little brother Janesh zooms around with his trucks, and various aunties are all yabbering away in Hindi and mainlining tea. But however full on it is, his mum, Asha, always has time for me. She bustles about, bracelets jangling, talking non stop and offering me food. She seems to think I'll starve to death unless she makes me eat at least two slices of cake and a handful of sticky, sugary Indian sweets. I'm not arguing. There isn't much in the way of sweetness at my house, I can tell you. Amil always tries to steer us straight up to his room and complains about the way she goes on. But I feel like the sun's beaming right down on me when she fusses and tells me how much I've grown and how handsome I'm getting, even though it's a bit embarrassing too. Sometimes it feels as though she likes me more than my own mum does.

Anyway, he comes out and we chat about this and that. Although I'm bursting to tell him what's been happening, I hold back. But as we reach the school gates, I can't keep it in any longer.

'Hey, Am, do something for me, will ya?'

'Look, man, you still owe me two quid from —'

'No, no, it's nothing like that,' I pause. 'I know this sounds weird, but I want you to . . . hit me.'

Amil stops and looks at me with an expression I'm seeing a lot lately. 'What are you on about, freak?'

'Do it! Go on. I'm testing something out.'

'If you insist.' Amil grins and then punches me in the gut. Hard.

I double over, trying to get my breath back. When I regain the power of speech I yell, 'That really hurt!'

Amil falls about laughing. 'What did you expect?' he says. 'You did ask!'

I swear at him quietly and we walk the rest of the way in silence. Amil shakes his head every now and then.

Me? I'm angry, humiliated and very, very confused.

I'm in history, and Mrs Jennings is droning on about some old rubbish or other. I'm looking out of the window and thinking about cracks and wondering how I am going to get the money for a new Xbox when . . .

' . . . so what's the answer, Callum?' says Jennings.

My head snaps round and I hear sniggers. Jennings is glaring at me. I try a winning smile, but she's immune to my charms.

'What is the answer to the question I just asked?' she repeats.

'Cheese?' It's the first thing that comes into my head.

The class erupts and I can't help dipping my head in a little bow.

'I'm glad you think that's funny,' says Jennings, stony-faced. 'I hope you enjoy doing an extra essay on the topic for me as much.'

She smiles at me then, evilly. 'I'd like it for the morning, please,' she says and turns back to point to the image on the white board.

'When the first flag was introduced in 1606,' she says to the class, 'it became known simply as the British flag or the flag of Britain'. She pauses and gives her head a weird shake. 'British flag or the flag of Britain,' she says again. Then she does the head shaky thing a second time. 'British flag or flag of Britain, flag of Britain, flag of Britain, flag of Britain . . .'

I look around the class, grinning. What's happened to the old cow? She's got stuck. Some people are scribbling frantically, but most are doodling or texting under the desk as usual. Even the people watching her have no expression other than the normal, bored one. The smile dies on my face as the horrible realisation takes hold.

I swallow hard. Is it only me who heard that? When I look back at Jennings, she's talking normally again.

I can't get out of the class fast enough at the end of the lesson. I gulp fresh air down and I'm clammy all over.

'What's up with you today, man?' says Amil.

I clutch his arm. He grins awkwardly and steps back a bit.

'Look, this is really important, right?' I say. 'So think carefully.'

He shakes my hand away with an embarrassed laugh. 'All right, but take it easy, yeah?'

I take a deep, slow breath. 'Did you hear Jennings repeat herself back there?'

Amil bursts out laughing. 'Course I did,' he says. 'Are you nuts?'

Relief pours into me. I could hug him. 'Thank God! I was starting to think I was really losing it, man!'

Amil laughs again. 'She always repeats herself, doesn't she?' he says. 'Different lessons, same old crap, innit?'

The warm feeling drains away, leaving behind a chill that feels like it will never go away.

I turn, trying to hide the scared look on my face. 'Yeah,' I say, quietly. 'Same old crap.'

Chapter 3

wires

'I've found a way for you to pay Ryan back,' says Des.

I look up from my dinner, trying to keep my expression blank but knowing I'm not going to like this.

'Yeah?' I say, through a mouthful of chips.

'It's through my mate, Loz,' he says and my heart falls as I picture the skinny, stoner freak with mad eyes Des sometimes works with. He's about a hundred and four, with ginger dreadlocks, and he's always hoiking huge phlegm bogies onto the ground.

'Right,' I say. My misery only adds to Desmondo's glee.

'Well, he's got a bit of work on at the moment renovating a building and you're going to help him. Pay's good – a tenner for evenings, twenty-five quid for weekends.'

'OK,' I say suspiciously. 'Where is it?'

Des puts half a sausage in his mouth and chews, grinning

the whole time so I can get the full chewing action. 'Not far. You can see it from here.'

'Aw, come on,' I say, 'I'm not having to work in the brewery with Pig—, Ryan, am I?'

'Nope,' says Des and spears the rest of the sausage, still grinning. 'Try again.'

'It's not school!' I say. 'I'm not working at the bloody school!'

'Not there either,' says Des. 'Try again!' He pauses but can't hold it in any longer. 'I'll tell you, then. It's Riley Hall! You should feel right at home among all those losers and toerags.' Des actually slaps his leg, he's so chuffed. 'Close your mouth, Princess, you'll catch flies,' he says, sitting back in his chair and letting out a massive burp.

I don't feel like the rest of my dinner but I keep going so he can't see how freaked out I am. He couldn't have given me worse news.

I've always had the horrors about Riley Hall. I can't explain why. I've never been there, but I only have to hear the name and I get this choking feeling. I have a recurring dream about it too, where I'm endlessly walking down corridors. All I can hear is a boy screaming in a room I never find.

Weird.

'So,' I say casually, which takes a truly impressive amount of effort. 'When do I start?'

'Tomorrow after school,' says Des. 'Make sure you get back here quickly.'

It gets worse every second. 'But I have art club on Wednesdays!'

Des leans across the table and lowers his voice. 'Not until you've paid for that Xbox you haven't.'

I try to swallow the rest of my dinner but it tastes like sand and polystyrene. Art club is one of the few places I feel like I'm any use. It's nothing to do with the fact that Miss Lovett, who takes it, is blonde and pretty and smells like she's just come out of the kind of frothy bath you see on adverts. And she says things like, 'That really is wonderful, Callum,' and 'I think you have a real aptitude for this,' which aren't words I hear anywhere else. I'd promised I'd help her paint some backdrops for a Year Eleven exhibition. Looks like I'm going to let her down.

I want to kick something. But I'm not giving Des the satisfaction.

After dinner, Mum's watching one of her soaps and Des is on the phone in the kitchen. Ryan's probably out torturing baby chicks or something. I'm sat on the sofa opposite mum, staring at a piece of paper with the words *Cal Conway, 9BF* at the top and nothing whatsoever about the stinking Union Jack or whatever the hell it's called. I'm thinking about everything that's been happening and suddenly Mum gets up. She moves to the middle of the room and in a voice that isn't really her own says, 'He can't be waking. It isn't possible. Increase the dosage by another five mils . . .'

'Mum? Mum, what are you doing?'

She turns her head and stares at me, still as a statue.

Des is still on the phone next door.

'Des!' I shout. 'Something's wrong with Mum!' Normally he'd yell at me for interrupting him. That's how I know, with another fizzing chill, that he can't hear me.

I jump up and stand in front of her, waving my hands about. But there's no reaction even though she's looking right at me. Her eyes are starey, like she's not even human. Then she abruptly flops back into her chair.

'What's the matter with you? Why are you gawping at me like that?' she says irritably.

I drop to my knees and cling onto her awkwardly, because I'm so scared and freaked out by everything. I can feel her body tighten but I hang on and squeeze harder. My head pulses with a sudden headache and I'm dizzy, so dizzy I cling tighter to Mum to stay upright.

'Cal, will you give over, you're hurting me!' She pushes me away and reaches for her fags, her face tight and annoyed. 'I don't know what's wrong with you at the moment, I really don't. Now get on with your homework and let me watch Corrie.'

I don't get any relief from worrying about all this at night-time. Oh no.

I already have a full repertoire of strange dreams. Not just the Riley Hall one. There's another, where I'm in a car, listening to the same nursery rhyme over and over again. Then everything goes scorching hot and I can't breathe. I've had that dream for as long as I can remember. But lately the two dreams are on shuffle.

I try to stay awake, listening to Pigface oinking in his sleep and sounds I don't want to hear from Mum and Des but eventually my eyes droop and now when I close them

I go hurtling down a Technicolor tube like a combination of the biggest rollercoaster and waterpark slide you can imagine. Except instead of it being a laugh, I'm fighting for my life. I see things exploding and body parts lying like joints of meat in a street. Ghostly white faces with no features lean over me, whispering harsh words I can't make out. I wake up coated in slimy sweat and feeling like I've done ten rounds in a boxing ring, my duvet strangling me.

There's a good dream too, though. It only comes now and then. I can see sunlight sprinkling the ground and I'm really high up. There are strong hands holding my legs and a little kid is laughing fit to bust. I think the little kid might be me. A woman with reddish hair is smiling up at me and reaches up to touch my face. I try to remember more because it feels good, like a warm bath, but it always stays just out of sight.

The next day after school I wait for Des's idiot mate to collect me. Telling Miss Lovett I wouldn't be at art club for the rest of term was bad, especially when I had to add the bit about not helping with the exhibition.

'Is there any way I could talk to your parents and we could reach a compromise?' she'd said, a lovely crease between her lovely brown eyes.

'No,' I said. 'I have to pay for something . . . something I broke.' I felt ashamed and suddenly angry, because she was making me feel bad.

'Well, maybe you can carry on with the picture you were

working on at home? It's so unusual, it would be a shame not to finish it.'

The picture she's talking about is of loads of wires. That's it, wires. They're snaking all over a room and a person is imprisoned in them, right at the centre.

Unusual is one word for it.

Anyway, I tried to picture myself at home, taking over the kitchen table with art stuff. Maybe Mum could say, 'Here's a nutritious snack, darling! You must keep up your energy levels for these marvellous artistic endeavours!' And then Des could come in, fart loudly and smack me round the back of the head for behaving like a girl. This made me angry too so I said, 'Nah, don't think so,' and walked out of the room without even saying goodbye or anything. I could feel her looking as I walked down the corridor and her gaze stayed on my back all day like a stain.

So I'm looking out the window, getting ready for Loz's arrival when Ryan comes into the kitchen with a sandwich in his hand. The other one is rummaging about in his trousers. He's home from work early for some reason and he stops dead when he sees me. His eyes narrow and I know he'll die before he forgives me for the other day.

'You know what they do in Riley, don't you?' he says.

'No, Ryan, why don't you tell me,' I say in a bored way.

He comes and stands over me so I feel his warm breath. 'They make weapons out of anything they get their hands on,' he says quietly. 'Bed springs, disposable forks, bits of plastic covering from the table.' His breathing is shallow like he's been running. 'Then they slice each other up with them. I reckon you'll be painting a wall and thinking your pathetic thoughts and the next thing, someone will come up behind you and open you up until you cry like a stuck pig.'

I swallow and I know he can see the fear in my eyes because his smile widens.

'So you'd better watch your back,' he whispers into my ear. 'And if they don't get you, I will. Only a matter of time.' He grins and moves away.

I hear a sound and look out the window. A battered white van, exhaust spewing a toxic brown cloud, parks in front of the house.

Ryan gives a snort and moves away to switch on the TV, while I pull on my trainers and think about how nice it would be if I were about to have all my teeth pulled out with a pair of broken pliers. Better than what I have to do now, anyway.

CHAPTER 4

sacrifice

Loz's van smells of feet, fags and dog. The mutt in question, a barrel of pure muscle and teeth, is called Tizer. He's tied up by a bit of string but I can feel his stinking breath on the back of my neck. If I turn, he rumbles like a washing machine about to spin.

Loz comes from Glasgow and I understand about a tenth of what he says. He mumbles into his chest and every now and then grins to show the little brown gravestones of his teeth.

He has a conversation into his mobile most of the way. Every now and then I catch something like, 'Wuzznae like that, hen,' or 'You're breakin' ma heart, darlin'!' I tune him out and stare at the sky, which is a weird pink colour. The clouds seem to be moving really fast. Do they usually look that way, like they're brewing something poisonous?

I suddenly can't remember what the sky normally looks like and that only adds to the battery acid feeling churning in my guts. The headache's back too. It comes and goes in a rhythm, squeezing my temples like a giant fist. I close my eyes for a minute and when I open them, the world stays dark for a scary second and then everything looks normal again.

Soon we're approaching a high barbed wire fence with a CCTV camera on massive metal gates.

You'd better watch your back.

Pigface's words come back to me and I unconsciously lean back in my seat, prompting a snarl from Tizer.

Loz roots around in his pocket and comes up with a dog-eared piece of paper. A tall guard glances at it and then we're driving up towards the main building.

If it looks grim from the top of the hill, close up it's downright scary.

Made from grey stone, it has hundreds of slitty windows that look like eyes peering down on you. Something about it feels really familiar but also makes me want to run away. My heart's beating like it's got a microphone strapped to it. I swear I can hear it all around me and I glance to check whether Loz has noticed, but he says nothing. For a minute I feel like I'll stop breathing if I have to go any further, which is so stupid because it's not like I've broken the law and got any reason to worry. It's this feeling I keep getting, that's all. Like if I go in there, I'll never get out again.

I clear my throat loudly and take a big breath. Got to get a grip on myself.

We reach another security entrance, where we have to walk through a metal detector. Another unsmiling guard pats us down all over our bodies, including between our legs, which is a bit embarrassing. He says, 'Right, come with me and I'll show you where to go and then I'll explain how to get back round with the van when it's been checked.'

Even Loz looks a bit nervous now and we trot behind the guard like pet dogs. I can hear lots of voices as well as the echoey sound of footsteps. It sounds a bit like school, except with no girl noises at all, and I miss them.

I glance up and see there are four levels with a wide open plan area in the middle. Boys of different ages, mainly late teens, are sitting around at tables, texting or playing cards and they all look at me and Loz as we walk by. One boy smiles nastily at me and then shouts, 'BOO!' at the top of his voice. I flinch and hear the mass hysteria that follows. Luckily we soon leave that area and go through a huge kitchen, filled with adults but also people I reckon are more inmates. It's hot and steamy and smells of old chip fat. Out the back there's another room that reeks of smoke.

The guard goes over to a window and pulls up a metal blind. Light floods in, revealing a room covered in black streaks. Dust is swirling around and there are bits of floating stuff in the air like black confetti that make me cough. I look up. There's some kind of metal air vent with cobwebs hanging from it.

The guard speaks. 'As you probably know, we had a fire in here. Most likely started by one of the lads working in the kitchen.' He pauses. 'We're not exactly short of arsonists here. So what we want is for it to be given a good clean before you paint it.'

There's a window on one side that looks over a court-yard, which has a basketball net and goal broken on one side with ripped netting. Probably an exercise area. I can see various lads hanging around in clusters. They all wear grey hoodies and one boy is standing in the opposite corner just facing the wall. But unlike the others, he has a huge X marked on his back. I wonder whether he's been picked out for something horrible. It gives me the creeps.

The guard clocks my expression. 'Don't worry,' he says, but not nicely. 'There's no access to this bit of the building from the yard. Water's over there.' He points to a filthy square sink to the left. There are cracks all over it that look like spider webs. 'Mops, buckets and cleaning stuff in the corner. OK?'

'Aye, right enough,' mumbles Loz and the guard nods before going out the way we came. We hear the sound of many locks being turned.

Loz goes and sits down on a chair in the corner and gets out his mobile. He glances up at me. 'Get on wi' it, then,' he says and starts furiously texting.

I look at the metal bucket propped up in the corner and, instead of filling it with water, I walk back over to the win-dow that looks over the exercise yard. At first I think the yard is empty now but then I realise the boy who was fac-ing the wall is still there. He's turned towards me but the grey hoodie is pulled down low, hiding his face. He's as still as a statue with his arms down and his palms facing out.

The word 'sacrifice' comes into my head for no reason at all. Adrenaline sizzles up my spine because I somehow know he's looking right at me. He's like a coiled spring and I imagine him suddenly leaping at the window. Then I give myself a little shake and tell myself to stop being such a muppet.

'Ye no started, yet?' Loz's voice makes me jump. Trying to hide my burning face, I hurry over to the sink and start clanking around with the bucket.

The next two hours are completely horrible. Loz keeps disappearing off for a cig or to make a phonecall and I'm left to do everything. Where the smoke hasn't reached, the corners are sticky with spilled food or crumby dust piles. I haul out one box and see tiny brown pellets that make my stomach heave. I want to ask Loz if he thinks there might be rats in here but know he'd only tell Des and they'd have a right laugh at my expense. I don't even have any rubber gloves and I decide that I'm not going anywhere near Rat Poo Corner until I've got a full chemical hazard suit on, or at least a pair of Mum's Marigolds.

After a lifetime, the guard comes back and looks around, frowning.

'Well, I hope you're going to work a bit faster than this,' he says and Loz looks genuinely offended even though he hasn't done a single stroke of work.

Soon we're outside in the fresh air, hearing the clunk of locks turning from inside. Loz doesn't say anything and we trudge back to the van.

Tizer is so excited at our return that he fills the car with toxic gas. Loz ruffles his ears like the dog has just done a trick and starts the engine. We're coming towards the main gates when I see something that makes me twist sharply in my seat.

'Whit's the matter wi' you?' says Loz.

'That boy,' I say, 'can you see him?'

He's standing right up against the inner fence with his hands outstretched, palms up. 'Course I can see him,' says Loz. 'Nasty wee neds, the lot of them.'

I don't answer. The boy had something on his hand . . . some sort of birthmark. I open my own palm and stare down at the identically shaped mark there. I give myself a shake. Stupid. It's just a coincidence. Right?

When I get back, a note on the kitchen table tells me Mum and Des have gone to the pub. Pigface seems to be having one of his mammoth sessions in the bog with his car mags.

I root about in the fridge and then make myself a doorstep sandwich. I eat the sarnie and then stare at my hand for ages. The birthmark is pinky brown and lozenge-shaped. Maybe loads of people have ones like this? It's a bit weird though . . . Pigface's mobile is on the table and it starts ringing. It doesn't go to voicemail and just rings on and on. Eventually it stops, then starts again. I don't know why I pick it up. I often don't know why I do the stupid things I do.

'Yeah?' I say.

'Who's this?' snaps a girl on the other end.

'Who's this?' I throw right back.

'It's Yasmine. Put Ryan on.'

Yasmine is the new woman in Pigface's life. Suddenly, my horrible new job and the fact that I'm going nuts and no one cares all come whizzing together and I find myself saying, 'Actually, Yasmine, didn't you know? He's gone out with Tanya White this evening.'

'He . . . *what?*'

'Yeah,' I go on, warming to the theme, 'I think he said he was taking her to the pub and then the new *Saw* movie.'

'The little . . .'

There are quite a few very unladylike words then and she hangs up. I stare at the phone. Then the toilet flushes and all the blood from my body seems to be replaced by iced water as I think about what I've done.

I hurry off to my bedroom and push a full chest of drawers up against the door. Mum's right, I'm an idiot and I don't help myself.

I hear sounds outside and can picture what's happening. Pigface sees he's got a missed call and then dials Yasmine's number. I know I've made a terrible, terrible mistake and, sure enough, a few minutes later I hear raised voices and I think about jumping out the window when there's an ear-splitting . . .

Bang Bang Bang!

. . . and Pigface is throwing his full weight against the door. I crawl backwards onto the bed and watch in horror as the doorframe actually starts to split apart. The chest of drawers is shifting sideways and I know that Pigface has gone way beyond the point of caring about the furniture. I throw open the bedroom window but have only just got my head out when I hear him burst into the room and his arms are round my waist dragging me back to the floor. He flips me over onto my back and squats over me, his eyes wild and a dangly bit of spit hanging off the side of his mouth like a rabid dog.

'Look, Ryan, it was only a joke! I didn't mean to —'

'Think you can make a monkey out of me, do you?' he screams and starts to punch me. The last thing I remember is reaching for the football trophy next to my bed and then there's nothing at all.

CHAPTER 5

gone

Voices come and go in surging waves and something's tugging at me. Not my body, but inside my head.

I say, 'Not yet, I'm not ready!' for some reason, and my eyes snap open.

It's morning. I'm in bed, fully clothed.

I can hear the radio on in the kitchen. I get up slowly, giving my ribs an experimental pat to see how bad they are. But they feel fine and when I pull up my T-shirt there are no bruises. I go into the kitchen and Mum's in there smoking and drinking a cup of tea. She looks up at me, but doesn't seem especially curious about anything.

'Tea in the pot,' she says, stubbing out her fag and patting the back of her hair.

I lean on the table as my words coming rushing out. 'Ryan beat me up! He could have killed me!'

She frowns, then smiles. 'What are you talking about, Cal?'

For God's sake! She's not going to believe me, is she? Either that, or Des will have persuaded her I was in the wrong. I can see them all sitting around the table discussing it, while I was out cold.

'You've got to believe me, Mum! He's completely out of control! He came into my room and started battering me and —'

Mum gives a funny laugh. 'Who did, Cal?' Like every word I've said was incomprehensible.

'Ryan!' I shout this time, unable to control myself a second longer. 'Bloody Ryan! He attacked me! He's out of control!'

Mum stops smiling. 'Cal, you've obviously had some kind of nightmare . . .' She pauses. 'You're not making any sense. Who's Ryan?'

Someone stops the clock.

I can hear every noise in the house, from the water in the pipes, to the gentle hum of the fridge.

I can hear Mum breathing and my own blood whooshing round my veins.

Maybe if neither of us speaks again, we can forget how mental this moment is and carry on as normal.

But instead I take a deep breath, swallow, and say, 'OK, not sure what's going on here but you know who Ryan is. He's Des's son, isn't he? You know, Desmondo? Lover boy? Your darling husband?'

Mum turns away and reaches for her handbag, shoving

her ciggies in the top. 'I don't know what's wrong with you this morning,' she says, 'but you'll be late for the programme if you don't hurry up.'

'Late for what programme?'

'Late for *school*, Cal! I said SCHOOL! Remember school? OK, there's my lift. Better get going!'

Chills zigzag up my neck. Mum walks briskly out the door. I run out behind her but she's already in a car that's puttering down the hill.

I'm shaking all over. My brain's hard drive is full. I can't take any more weirdness. I haven't got room. I look around the kitchen. Shock spikes in my belly again because I know something is different but I can't put my finger on it.

And then I realise.

Des's chair isn't here. It's an old battered armchair where he likes to sit in the morning and drink his tea. There are none of his sweatshirt tops lying around either and no copy of yesterday's *Sun* where he normally leaves it next to the kettle.

There's nothing of his in the kitchen whatsoever.

And I'll tell you what else is missing. I can't see any of Pigface's stuff lying around. I scan the room again. The picture on the wall above the telephone – the one of Des and Mum on their wedding day – has gone. Instead, there's a painting of a vase of flowers. It's a different size to the wedding picture and I move it to one side and can see the right-sized mark on the wall, telling me this one has always been in that spot.

I run into Mum's bedroom. It looks normal but when I

throw open the wardrobes, they're empty. Are they all leaving home? Is that it? Weren't they even going to tell me? My eyes sting. Well, stuff the lot of them. I'd rather live here on my own.

But then I hear something. A woman's crying somewhere in the house. There's something else . . . a police car siren outside. And it's getting closer. The sounds stop, abruptly, and all I can hear is my own heartbeat. Where have they gone? I try to picture family friends or someone I can ask. But it's like trying to watch a broken television. Panic's rising inside me and I'm drowning. I try to clutch at any memory. Last year, last week? But I can't remember anything that happened before the last couple of days. Not Christmas or birthdays or anything.

Nothing before I saw that crack in the ceiling of the boys' bogs.

I look down at my hands, needing reassurance that I'm at least real. The strange pin-pricks of light are there again. I shove my hands hard into my pockets, shaking all over.

'Not real, not real, not real,' I whisper. I have to get out of this house right now. School. I'll go to school, just like normal. Schools don't disappear even when you want them to.

I run out of the house and head down the hill.

'It's all right, see?' I murmur to myself. 'I'm fine. Just fine.'

But the cracks aren't done with me yet.

CHAPTER 6

cracks

I'm halfway down the hill when there's a rumbling under my feet and the road starts to judder and shake. The ground creaks and groans and then the hillside splits open like it's being pulled apart by giant hands. Brown earth churns up and I fall back onto my bum, whimpering a bit as a huge crack races like fire down the hill. It spreads across the outside of the brewery and the tall chimneys fold over slowly and crumple before the whole building collapses into a giant hole in the ground. The roaring and tearing fill my head like the scream of something being murdered but then there's silence. No birds, no cars. Silence, apart from my heavy breathing and that pounding heartbeat again that feels like it's outside me and all around.

The school goes next, folding with an enormous roar. The old red bricks release a massive cloud of dust. I don't mind admitting that I'm crying, thinking about all the people who must be inside by now like Amil and Miss Lovett and even Peters and Jennings who might be pains in the arse but never deserved to die, not crushed beneath a pile of bricks. I start running faster towards the school. I might be skinny but I'm strong and fast from training. Maybe I can dig some people out with my hands before the emergency services get here . . .

. . . and then I stop. Surely there should be fire engines on their way to the two disasters? People screaming from the wreckage? Even if every last person was killed inside, there are shops and houses round the school. Why aren't there people rushing out to help or even just to rubberneck? The headache comes back suddenly. There's a dull knocking inside my skull that makes me groan and put my fingers to my forehead. Did something hit me in the earthquake? I can't feel any bumps. The birthmark on my hand though . . . it's even clearer than usual. Darker and brighter all at once.

Maybe this is all some kind of massive joke and in a minute someone with a camera is going to jump out and then put me on YouTube. A hysterical barking laugh comes out of me and I force my mouth closed, because I sound nuts.

I walk down the road a bit further and jump at the sight of a black and white cat on a wall, licking its paws and staring right at me. It's the one I saw before. I rub under its chin and it vibrates all over like it's motorised.

'What now, puss?' I'm shaking hard and my teeth are chattering. I want to hold the cat close and curl into a ball until someone makes things normal again. I won't complain any more, I promise. Des and Pigface can boot me all over the place and I won't moan. I just want this weirdness to stop. I walk around in a circle for a moment, thinking. Where to go? Where to go?

I catch sight of an ugly grey building in the distance. It's the only thing on the horizon now the school and factory have gone. My feet start taking me towards it.

I don't know why I'm heading to Riley Hall. It's the place that scares me most. But I can't seem to stop myself. It's like I'm going to find an answer there; an answer to a question I don't even know yet.

I walk past silent houses and shops and cafés where lights are on and music plays but no one is home. The cat follows, jumping from one gate post to the next and then padding along behind me with its little white-socked paws. I stop and rub its warm head, grateful for its heartbeat and warm, furry life.

The main gate to Riley Hall is wide open. I thought I'd lost the capacity to be shocked today but once I step through, the gate slams closed behind me and I nearly wet my pants. The cat mewls at me from outside the gate.

'Sorry, puss.'

Leaving it behind feels like the worst thing I've ever done. I have to bite on my hand to stop the violent shivers shuddering through me like electric shocks. I walk up to the main building. The door's open, of course. Inside, I think I can hear echoes – ghostly voices and clanging of metal doors, shouts, snatches of radio but then . . . silence.

It looks different from last time. There's no open plan area now. Instead it's made up of long corridors with closed doors, just like in my dreams. I walk slowly down the first corridor and somewhere I can hear *beep, beep, beep* in the distance. I look up and jump because the boy I saw before is standing at the end of the corridor, his hood pulled low over his face. He turns and walks quickly away from me.

'Hey!'

But he ignores me and just hurries on, head bent. A noise behind makes me spin round. The wall is painted a dirty light green and pockmarked all over with graffiti and small holes but now a crack's formed that spreads and branches out all over. I stumble away from it as the wall groans and a huge hole appears in the middle. I can hear the wind whistling through the gap but I feel like I'm stuck to the ground. A hand appears around the side of the hole and a face appears, grinning.

It's Pigface. His eyes are devil red and his grinning mouth is bigger and wider than any human mouth should be. 'I've come to get you,' he says and his voice is so deep it rumbles through my whole body.

I cry out and start running down the corridor. I can hear the bricks falling as he climbs through the hole and I'm running harder than I've ever run before. I get round the corner and see the hoodie boy again.

'Hey,' I shout, 'help me!' But he carries on walking, head down and hands in pockets.

I run faster from Pigface's pounding footsteps behind me.

'I'm coming to get you, Cal!' His voice has slowed down to a terrible drawl.

The boy opens a door near the end of the corridor and disappears through it. I run after him, praying it will open, and it does. I fumble with the lock on the inside of the door and can hear Pigface's fists thump against it in frustration.

The boy is facing a big window with his back to me.

'Hey!' I shout but he ignores me. His shoulders start heaving up and down like he's laughing or crying. I can't tell which. Light blazes into the room so the edges of him are all fuzzy and undefined. Maybe he's got a knife. Maybe he'll turn round and plunge it straight into me. But I want to see his face. Talk to him. I can't seem to get near though; it's almost like I'm walking on the spot. I start running as fast I as can, my feet slamming against the stone floor.

Sharp pains creep up my arms and legs. I can't get my breath now and my lungs pull and strain for air. A voice whispers something right next to me.

'Who's there?' I gasp, spinning round to look but there's no one else in the room. It's just me and the boy. A harsh *beep, beep, beep* starts up all around until I think my eardrums are going to pop like balloons. Suddenly, the noise stops and everything goes silent. The boy turns round.

And I'm looking into my own face.

Part II

CHAPTER 7

the facility

I'm in deep water. I want to stay here but I can't stop myself from soaring upwards towards the surface. There's an explosion of light and sound and I gasp as I break the skin. My mouth feels like an animal died in it and there's a horrible sick smell around me.

I'm huddled in the corner of a room looking up at a face. The face belongs to a man who's thin and pale, with glasses. He's bald. He smiles and stretches out a hand but something seems to shrivel inside me and I don't want to touch him for some reason.

'Welcome back, Callum. You've been away a long time,' he says in a posh, deep voice.

I gawp and try to speak but all that comes out is a croaking sound. I try again.

'What happened?' My voice sounds rusty, like it hasn't

been used for ages, and my throat hurts like mad.

The man gestures with his hand. 'Let's get you on your feet and then I can answer your questions.'

I'm wearing hospital-like clothes and I can feel my hair is hanging down around my collar. How long have I been here? I get unsteadily to my feet and look around.

Along with Baldy there's another bloke, younger, with a beard, wearing blue hospital scrubs. I'm in a room that looks like it hasn't been used for ages. There are piles of boxes and a mop in an old bucket, just like the one I used at Riley Hall.

I have so many questions but I can't get my mouth to work properly. A wave of nausea swirls inside me.

'Steady,' says the other man but I bend over and puke all over the shoes of Baldy, who yelps and jumps back.

'Sorry,' I mumble.

'It's fine,' says Baldy, shaking the sick off his shoe with a grimace. 'Let's get you cleaned up, Callum.'

'Cal,' I say, even though it's about the least important thing I could possibly say at this moment. 'It's Cal.'

I don't know what will happen next. Dogs could start talking and it could rain pink frogs right now. It wouldn't be stranger than what's already happening.

'Right,' says the man. 'Let's get you back to your room and we can talk.'

My room? My *room*?

'Where am I?' I say at last.

'Well, at the moment you're in an old storeroom. Looks like you went on a walkabout. We had some trouble finding you this morning. But I'll explain properly when we get you back to your room, as I said.'

OK, now I get it. I went mad, just like I thought, and got myself locked in a loony bin. I bet Des loved it when they carted me away.

I dumbly follow them out of the storeroom and down a long, plain corridor with closed doors on both sides.

Smells are assaulting me from every angle. Disinfectant, food, and even aftershave from the man, are all so strong I want to gag. And everything is too bright. I squint up and see small lights buried into the ceiling.

'Where am I?' I say again and my small voice makes me sound about five years old.

The men exchange glances and open a door at the end of the corridor.

Inside is a plain white room which feels familiar. I look around, so confused and dizzy I can't speak. The ground tilts sideways and I feel the impact of the ground rushing to meet me just as everything shrinks to a tiny pinhole.

More voices.

'Do you think he can hear us?'

'I don't know. We should be cautious about what we say. Everything's changed. There are no protocols for any of this so we have no way of knowing his level of awareness post cracks.'

'When can we continue?'

'Shh, I think he's . . .'

I force my eyes open.

This time I'm lying on top of a bed. The bearded man is standing over me and a woman in blue scrubs is facing away. She turns around. I gasp so hard it hurts my throat.

'*Mum?*'

She stares back at me, frowning. Then I realise it's not Mum at all. I feel like someone has punched me in the guts. She looks a bit like Mum but is loads younger and more done up. I can smell her perfume and even the sickly sweetness of her make-up.

She's wearing a stethoscope round her neck. She comes over and gently eases me back against the pillow. I smell toothpaste and coffee on her breath.

'I'm just going to listen to your heart, Callum,' she says. 'You probably feel a little disorientated so try not to speak for a minute.' Her voice is nothing like Mum's. She sounds completely different. I'm so confused I just stare hard into her face as she bends over me. I feel tears spill over my eyelids and one slips over my cheek and goes hotly into my ear. But she doesn't really look at me.

'It's Cal,' I whisper. But no one is listening.

The door swings open and the bald man from before strides in. His smile doesn't reach his eyes as he comes and stands at the side of the bed. He exchanges a look with the nurse and she leaves the room. Her thick-soled shoes make a shushy sound on the floor.

'I want to know what's going on,' I say and try to swallow tears. 'I don't know where I am. I want to go home.'

'Sit up, Callum,' he says, 'and we can talk properly.'

'I told you already, it's *Cal!*' I want to shout it but my

voice doesn't work properly still.

'Sorry, I'll try to remember,' he says. His smile is tight as a drum.

I sit up again and a sharp sweat smell wafts up. As Baldy comes closer, I catch a whiff of his milky cereal on his breath. Cheerios, I'm sure it's Cheerios. Everything stinks here. And it's so bright. I groan and raise my hand to shield my eyes from the glaring lights overhead.

He gestures to the beardy male nurse and the light dims. 'Is that better?' he says and I nod.

He pulls a plastic chair from the side of the room and sits on it back to front. 'I'm Dr Daniel Cavendish,' he says. 'You're in a special research unit . . . a hospital, I guess you could say. We call it the Facility.'

Loony bin. Definitely.

'Was it because of the cracks? Is that why I was brought here?'

He glances at Beardy with a puzzled expression before his eyes flick back to me. He hesitates for a second before speaking again. 'I'm not quite sure . . . um, how to . . .'

I have a very strong urge to punch this bloke. Why won't he just tell me what's going on? How long have I been in this place, anyway?

'Well, why don't you just tell me when I came here?' I say as he continues to stare. 'Is it still Thursday? It's Thursday, right?'

Cavendish swallows, visibly. 'You've been here for rather longer than you might realise,' he says.

'Oh,' I say. 'How long, then?'

His eyes flick around again. I get a weird mental image of a lizard with a long tongue, lassoing flies. He hesitates for ages before speaking. 'You've been here for twelve years.'

CHAPTER 8

unexpected effects

The room tips sideways. The beardy male nurse quickly shoves a cardboard bowl under my chin. I gag but nothing comes up. A pounding in my head seems to echo around the walls.

'Twelve *years*?'

Why would he say something so *stupid* and *wrong*?

Both men stare back at me, their expressions blank.

'Twelve years?' I say again, more quietly this time. 'Are you mad? Is this a joke?'

Cavendish crosses one leg over the other. 'I know it's difficult to absorb right now. You were brought here, injured, as a small boy,' he says. 'You'd been in a car accident.' He pauses. 'Your injuries were very serious. You almost died.'

I think my jaw actually drops open.

Cavendish continues. 'We decided to attempt an

experimental neurological procedure.' Pause. 'Brain surgery.' Pause. 'And it saved your life. But there were some unexpected effects.'

'What do you mean, *unexpected effects*?'

He exchanges glances with the other man again. He talks like he has the worst constipation ever. Stop, start, strain; stop, start, strain.

'Well . . . technically you were in a coma,' says Cavendish, 'but you could move freely. All tests showed your brain activity was strong but you were living in a world inside your own mind.'

It's not raining pink frogs but it might as well be for all the sense he's making.

'What, you mean . . . I was dreaming?'

'No, not dreaming,' he says, leaning forward. 'Brain scans showed you were in a coma. Coma patients may twitch or have muscle spasms, but they are unable to use their limbs. You were the first ever to actually get up and move around.'

'But I've been here the whole time? I was like that for years and years? Why didn't anyone take me home? What about my parents . . . family?'

Silence. Then . . . 'We've never been able to trace anyone. Sorry. You have no living family that we're aware of.'

No. That can't be true. There must be someone who cares about me. Mustn't there?

A big silence fills the room, pushing all the oxygen out. There's too much to ask. I can't make the space for the questions in my head, let alone get them out properly. 'Why *did* I wake up then?' I squeeze my nails into my palms to stop myself from freaking out.

Cavendish clears his throat. 'We're not sure exactly why it happened now. You've been emerging for the last week but all we could do was watch and wait.'

I don't know why, but a crazy laugh barks from my mouth and I have to squeeze my fists even tighter. My legs are trembling so hard my knees are bouncing up and down. All I want to do is get up and run. Anywhere. Somewhere this isn't happening any more.

'So, what?' I say through gritted teeth. 'I've just knocked about in this room like some kind of zombie for twelve years? That's nuts. You're nuts!'

'It wasn't exactly like that,' says Cavendish in that oily, patient voice. 'You were moving about inside your own world. We've watched and studied you and carried out constant tests. The work here has helped us to make huge advances in neurology. But you haven't been lying in bed all that time, if that's what you're thinking. Here, I'll show you.'

Cavendish gestures to Beardy, who walks over to the far wall and presses a button. There's a whirring sound and the walls splits into two parts, revealing a kind of glass pod hanging from the ceiling like a giant egg. I swing my legs round to the side of the bed. Beardy goes to stop me but Cavendish puts a hand on his arm and shakes his head warningly. I walk a bit unsteadily over to the pod. I've never seen it before, but I know it all the same. I lean my forehead against the cool glass and look inside. I can see hundreds of tiny pinpoints of light. I look down at my own hands instinctively.

I've seen them. The lights on my skin.

And that's the horrible moment when I know for certain this isn't just a bad dream.

This is real.

'What is this thing?' I croak, closing my eyes for a second as another sicky wave hits my stomach.

'It's a suspension pod,' says Cavendish. 'When you weren't in your bed, it allowed you to move, to run, to stay fit, without becoming injured. You were locked inside your own mind but your body was – is – healthy. This just kept you safe.'

I stare into the pod numbly. Can this tiny space really have been my whole world for twelve years? I can't take it in. It's too much. I don't want to be here. I want to be on the sofa watching telly at home with a jumbo bag of crisps next to me on the sofa. I won't complain about Des or Ryan or school or anything ever again. I just want things back how they were.

Is he saying none of that ever happened?

A big babyish feeling rises up and I squeeze my burning eyes shut so I don't start blubbing everywhere. Questions. Must ask questions. Got to pick it all to bits until it makes sense.

'So how did I end up in that room?' I say, turning back to face Cavendish and Beardy again. 'Where I woke up?'

They exchange glances. It feels like there is another, unspoken conversation going on here.

'Your room door is usually kept closed for your own safety,' says Cavendish in a tight voice. 'But someone . . . left it open this morning. In error.'

Images of the room in Riley Hall flash into my mind. The boy . . . he was just a twisted sort of a dream, then. But what about the others?

'So how do you explain all the people I know?' I say. I know I'm speaking too loudly now because Cavendish winces. Tough. 'What about school? What about Mum and Des and Pigface? I didn't just make them up! I have a history! A family!'

Cavendish clears his throat. 'We don't exactly know how your mind created the world it did. But the vivid details may have something to do with the procedure you underwent.' He pauses again. 'Your original surgery involved transplantation of brain tissue from a donor.'

'A donor?' I say, stupidly.

'Yes . . . You received brain tissue from a local boy who died on the day you came here.' He pauses. 'Memory is a complex thing and there is no scientific reason why memories couldn't be transplanted from one person to another but . . .'

'What are you on about?'

He shifts again. 'The part of the brain we transplanted is known as the amygdala and among other things it helps control memory. And . . . the boy in question may also have had a mother, stepfather and so on. I think you may have been reliving some of his memories.'

I pause for just one second and then I'm shouting. 'So

why does that nurse look like my mum?'

Cavendish's looking at me like I'm a dangerous dog. 'Do try to stay calm.'

'Don't tell me to be calm!' I yell.

Cavendish swallows again. He has a huge Adam's apple that bobs up and down above his collar. 'You've been living somewhere between consciousness and unconsciousness,' he says. 'Your brain has simply woven details from real life into your coma state.'

No . . . It's not fair. I want to curl into a ball or howl and cry and hit someone.

None of it was real? Not Mum, or home, or Amil or school? Could they really be just someone else's memories, all mashed together with stuff happening around me here in this room? I look around at the plain white walls and the horrible pod in the corner, then at Cavendish, Beardy and the nurse. I think about the beeping sounds in my head and when Pigface couldn't hit me that time.

'Sometimes it seemed like —' I close my mouth, biting the words back.

'Like what?' says Cavendish quietly.

I hesitate. 'Like things weren't real.'

He nods. 'I expect this was when you were closest to regaining consciousness.'

I suddenly remember Mum, or whoever she was, sliding across the floor in that weird way with blank eyes. What was it she said? 'He can't be waking up?' and then something about increasing the dosage? I don't understand why they'd say that. They must have wanted me to wake up, surely?

I stare at Cavendish until he blinks, twice in a row, and then I look away. It's probably all got mixed up inside my head. It's not like they'd have any reason for keeping me in a coma. I can't make sense of anything right now.

'How did he die?' I croak at last.

'Who?' says Cavendish.

'The boy. The one whose memories I'm carrying in my head.' Just saying those words makes me want to throw up or scratch myself all over. I feel like I've been invaded by insects.

'I'm not sure of the exact details,' says Cavendish, 'but it was a long time ago. I suspect it was an accident of some sort. He's not important now, anyway.'

Not important?

I want to go home.

I have no home.

I want to go home.

'Can I go there?'

Cavendish looks at the other guy again. 'Where?' he says.

'The house on the hill. The house where I, where he, where they all live. I want to go there.' I know I'm not making sense.

Cavendish tips his head back a little, frowning. He clears his throat. 'If you mean a place from your coma world, that would be a mistake, even if you could locate where it was in the real world. Your mind has had to cope with a lot, Cal. Best just to start again and forget about the past.'

'*If* I could locate it!' I almost laugh and then realise I

can't remember the address of the house on the hill any more. It's gone. I swallow and squeeze the thin blanket in both fists like I'm clinging on to the edge of the world.

'Why a mistake?' I say.

'What?'

'Why would it be a mistake to go there?'

Cavendish runs his tongue over his dry lips and I catch a whiff of his breath again, sour now under the milky smell.

'Uh . . . well, there's a serious risk that it could result in some kind of cerebral overload. Either a stroke, or a major psychological trauma that could be just as dangerous. Mixing the two realities – the world of your coma and the real world – is just not advisable. These are such unusual circumstances. Anything could go wrong.'

I sink back onto the bed and cradle my head in my hands. I feel like my whole world has been picked up and shaken like one of those glass snowstorms.

The silence seems to go on for ever.

'What happens to me now?' I say finally through a headful of snot. 'Where will I go?'

'As I said, we've never managed to trace any family, I'm afraid,' says Cavendish. 'But do try not to worry about the future at the moment. You'll need a period of recovery. We'll have to monitor you to make sure there are no after-effects of the coma.' He gets up. 'You should rest now. Try to get some more sleep.'

He moves so quickly I don't see what he's doing until I feel a prick in my hand. 'Just to help you relax,' he says and I see he's holding a syringe.

I can feel myself falling, but before I do, a question bubbles out of me.

'How did you know that Des was my stepdad?' I start to say. 'I didn't tell you that . . .' but the words just echo inside my own head.

Chapter 9

window bars

Time passes but I don't know how many days or nights because they all bleed into one. I can't seem to stop sleeping. I don't dream, but every time I wake up, my new reality washes over me like cold water.

'You're nothing . . . nobody.'

That's what Des – or whoever he really was – said. Maybe he was right.

Because it doesn't seem like anyone cared about me that much either, if they left me here to rot all that time. It feels like Des and Tina and even Pigface would be better than being some sort of walking blank page. My insides hurt but I know it's nothing to do with after-effects of being in the coma. It's an ache for what I thought was my life.

I keep going over what I can remember but there's

nothing before the cracking ceiling in the boys' toilets. I have a theory, though: I reckon this was when I was starting to wake up. I've asked Cavendish for details about the crash again and how I got here but he keeps saying he has nothing more to tell me. I wonder about what happened all the time. Who was driving the car? I must have had parents somewhere down the line. Did they love me, like proper parents? But if they did, how could they have let me stay here so long? Did they die in the car crash? And then I start thinking about the dead donor boy and wondering who he was. I feel like he's here, somewhere inside me, all the time. Which is pretty creepy and horrible when you think about it. Who wants to have a dead person inside them, even if it is just a bit of bodily tissue?

They bring me tablets but they make me feel sick and drowsy so I pretend to take them, hiding them between the mattress and the fitted sheet.

One morning I wake up and I realise I've had enough of the pity party in my head. I need to do something. I stink, as much as anything. There's a bathroom next door but I've only used the toilet until now. I've been avoiding the round mirror above the sink, like it's a portal that will take me somewhere bad. If I look like a different boy to the one I think I am, I really will go nuts.

I throw back the sheets before I can change my mind and march straight in there. Putting my hands on the sink with my head bent, I count to three . . . and force myself to look up.

I make a little noise in my throat. My knees go and I

slump forwards. I have to take deep breaths. Relief is melting all my bones to warm jelly. Once I've got a grip on myself, I look again.

Dirty blond sticky-out hair? Longer than normal, but check. Dark brown eyes? Check. Mole on right cheek? Check.

So far, so me.

I glance down quickly at my hand. I still have the birthmark: a small oval stain on my palm. I take off my musty pyjama top and check myself out properly. It's weird, but I look like I really have been training. I flex my fist and look at the sinewy ropes on my arm. I can't make any sense of it, but I'm grateful. I probably need all the strength I've got right now.

I get into the shower. All the stuff they told me about comas and brain tissue makes me feel sort of itchy and dirty so I let the hot water run over me for ages, like I can wash away twelve years of lies. A sudden thought makes me gasp, accidentally inhaling some water. How did I get clean before? Did they wash me? I want to punch a hole through the glass but I'm too busy spluttering. It's not just the water. The shower gel is so piney-strong it makes my nose ache and tickle. My old world is fading fast but I know it was never this brightly lit or as smelly as the real world. It's like my senses have woken up for the first time and are all doing overtime. Now I'm awake, that other world in my head feels like a faded old photo.

After my shower, I find some clothes neatly folded on the

bed. They look old but smell clean. I pull on a plain white T-shirt and some jeans that seem to be the right size. No shoes though and that's a pain. How do they expect me to go anywhere without shoes?

Anyway, once dressed, I'm starving. I've only picked at the odd sandwich or bowl of cereal left in my room until now. I wasn't hungry and my throat hurt. But suddenly I feel like I could eat a scabby donkey if it came with fries. Some toast and jam has been left out for me. The toast is so toasty and the jam so jammy that the flavours make me dizzy. I can't help folding a whole piece into my mouth at once.

'Steady there,' says Beardy. I hadn't noticed him come in. They all do that. None of them knock. 'You might want to take that a bit slower.'

I take a huge slurp of juice, which tastes like sunshine in a glass. It's such orange heaven I just stare at it for a moment in awe. Something occurs to me.

'Hey,' I say, 'could I eat properly? When I was in the coma?'

Beardy is starting to clear the breakfast stuff away. He's barely given me any eye contact so far and doesn't look at me now. None of them are friendly. It feels like they don't know what to do with me now I've woken up. Like they preferred me when I was a boy in a pod who didn't ask questions.

'Yes,' he says hesitantly, 'technically you could. But it was thought best that we stuck with tube feeding most of the time.'

I swallow and put the glass down. I'm not so thirsty now. I understand why my throat hurt and my voice was croaky. My hand instinctively goes to my neck.

Beardy's walking towards the door.

'Wait!'

He stops.

'Am I really named Cal?' Maybe it was the other boy's name . . . the dead one. A wave of panic washes over me in case I don't even know what I'm really called.

'I believe so, yes,' he says and starts to leave the room.

'Hey?'

This time his expression is definitely irritated.

'So do you know my surname as well?'

He doesn't answer straight away. 'I'm not sure about that. I've only been here for a few months,' he says, looking away. 'Maybe you should ask Dr Cavendish.'

He bustles out of the room and I lean back against my pillows, weak with relief that at least my name is my own. Despite living that weird, borrowed life inside my head, some little part of me must have hung onto my real identity. But I'd still like to know why they're so sure. If they know my name, maybe they know a bit more about where I came from? I decide I'm going to pump Cavendish to tell me every tiny detail of what he knows later.

First I want to get a proper look at where I've been living for the last twelve years. It's crazy, but I haven't even looked outside the window yet. I yank up the beige venetian blinds covering the window. That's weird. There are thick metal bars across it and rolls of vicious spikes curling along the window sill. Rain is running down the window but I can't hear it at all. These windows are seriously thick. Outside there's a car park flanked by a high perimeter wall, also covered in rolls of barbed wire and metal spikes. A lone guard in a long waterproof coat with a hood is walking up and down with a huge Alsatian dog, a rifle slung over his shoulder.

Why the OTT security? I feel dizzy as a pin sharp memory of being inside Riley Hall flashes across my mind. It's not like I'm a prisoner here. It's completely different. Right? So what would happen if I just made my way to the front door and walked out? I'm a free citizen. I can do what I want. For some reason though, my heart thrums hard against my ribcage as I poke my head outside the door. I start walking.

At the end of the corridor I see Cavendish talking to another man, a real bruiser with pock-marked skin and shoulders as wide as an American footballer. He pushes the jacket of his blue suit back to adjust his belt and I spy a gun there, nestled against his waist. I draw back behind a large metal trolley filled with cleaning equipment. Cavendish is speaking in an animated way and if he's intimidated by a bloke that size who's tooled up, he isn't showing it. If anything, the other bloke has his palms up as though he's apologising about something. I creep down the corridor in the other direction and pass a room where some men dressed in dark blue uniforms – something between a policeman and a soldier's uniform – are leaning over a table. I pause for just long enough to see that the table is loaded with machine guns and the men casually pick them up as though they're nothing.

I quicken my pace, heart banging almost painfully now.

I'm looking back over my shoulder to check I'm not being followed as I hurry round the next corner. And slam straight into Beardy.

'Where are you going?' He puts his hand on my arm. His eyes and voice are cold as ice.

'Just a walk,' I say, trying to strike the exact right balance between casual and not-to-be-messed-with.

Beardy's eyes dart about and he licks his lips. 'It's not a good idea to go wandering,' he says. 'You're still quite weak. Come on, back to your room.' He takes me by the arm again and I try to shrug him off but his grip is strong.

'But I'm not weak!' I say. 'I feel fine!'

'That's as maybe,' he says, 'but you don't know what's best for you right now. You need to rest.'

Within about four seconds I'm back in my room. I hear a key turning in the lock.

I pace about furiously. This is all wrong. Why won't they let me go where I want? And what's with all the guns? I try a few experimental bangs on the door but no one comes.

Ages later, two female nurses come in, locking the door after them. Without saying anything or looking at me they start putting together a tray with syringes and stuff on it. I've had enough. I snatch a syringe from the trolley and hold it to my throat.

'Go get Cavendish,' I say, 'or I'm going to stick this in my neck and you'll have to explain it to him. *Do it!*'

I must look crazy enough because the two nurses look nervously at each other and one scurries out of the room. Seconds later, Cavendish comes bustling through the door.

'Just put that down, Cal, and we can talk. You could hurt yourself.'

'I want to know why I'm locked in,' I say and he approaches slowly, nodding. 'And I want to know everything you know about me. About who I am.'

'OK! OK . . . Please, Cal, you could hurt yourself. If you'll just put that down we can talk. Please?'

I feel a bit stupid, to be honest, so I drop the syringe onto the trolley.

Cavendish visibly relaxes. 'Right, thank you. Sit down, Cal.'

'I'll stand, thanks.' I lean against the wall and cross my arms.

He sighs and then sits down on the end of the bed. 'First of all, what we do here is not just any old research,' he says. 'We're at the very cutting edge of neuro-technology.' He clocks my baffled expression. 'That is, technology as it relates to brain science and the study of consciousness.' He brushes a bit of dust from his immaculately pressed trousers and leans closer. 'We don't publicise what we do, because much of our work involves confidentiality of patients, but inevitably information sometimes gets out. The fact is we've had a security breach. There's an organisation that wants to disrupt our work and we discovered that someone working here, one of our nurses, was involved. They are criminals who are against the work we do. They want to turn the clock back. They spread lies and propaganda about our organisation.'

'What kind of lies?'

He blinks. 'They're just fanatics. Extremists. They really shouldn't concern you because you are perfectly safe here. We just have to protect our patients and our valuable technology and, sadly, that can necessitate high security.'

'But why lock me in?'

There's the briefest pause. 'We're carrying out a security check. Please don't be concerned. It shouldn't take long.'

I take a deep breath. 'OK. So how come you know my name is Cal? What's my surname? What else do you know about me?'

Cavendish runs his tongue across his lips. His expression is weird and he keeps blinking. 'Your full name is . . .' He hesitates, as though making a decision. 'Callum Conway. There will have been paperwork. I'll have to look at our records.' He looks at me. 'You shouldn't really be out of bed yet. Have you been taking the medication we've been giving you, Cal?'

I go cold inside. 'Yeah,' I lie. 'Why?'

'Just checking. I'll be back later, OK?' He practically runs out of the room and I hear it lock again.

I prowl the room, feeling like a caged animal. Something feels wrong here. I think Cavendish knows more than he's letting on. I start pulling open the drawers in the bedside cabinet, although I don't really know what I'm looking for. It's just something to do while I try to think. He was very keen for me to be taking those pills, but what was in them? I think they were stopping me from being alert. I need my wits about me.

I pull out another drawer. The first two were empty but the bottom one contains a pad of lined paper and an old pencil. I stare at them for a minute then sit down on the bed. I rest the pad against my drawn up knees and my hand starts sketching before my brain even registers what I'm doing. It's just something to stop me from climbing the walls until I can get some answers. I liked drawing in that old world. I quickly realise I'm pretty good in this one too. The movement of my hand as the pencil crosses the page, quick and fluid, makes me feel calmer inside. I draw the house on the hill as I remember it, filling in all the details like the old tyres and Des's precious shed. Then I draw the school but with a cartoon curvy version of Miss Lovett standing outside it, hand on her hip and blowing a kiss. This makes me smile for what must be the first time since I came round.

Then I draw the newsagent's that Amil's mum and dad owned, crammed with magazines and newspapers and rows and rows of sweets. There's a distinctive sign with swirly writing that says *The Sweet Stop*. It's so clear in my mind, I can picture it exactly. It's so weird to think I've never been there. How can this be someone else's memory and not mine? It's insane. Then something else comes to me. The shop is called that because it's right next to a train station! I close my eyes for a minute and a whole series of images flit across my mind. I can see a war memorial in the shape of a cross. And then a sign appears as vividly as though someone has shown me a photograph.

It says, *Welcome to Brinkley Cross.*

My heart starts to pound and I swallow hard. This is it, this is where the boy came from and where all my fake memories were made. Maybe I can go back there and find out who he was. And that might be a step towards finding out who I am too. I think about Cavendish saying it would be dangerous. Would it be too risky to try?

The light bleeds out of the room but I sit there for ages, just thinking.

After a while, I lie down on the bed, letting my thoughts drift. I still feel really tired, even though I'm not taking the dodgy pills. But I feel as though there's some vague plan inside me now. I curl up and start imagining all sorts of daft things, like Amil's mum and dad adopting me. I can almost taste those yummy pink sweets. I drift into sleep, dreaming about a new life and starting again with real friends and a real family who love me. It's warm and safe and I sigh deeply. Sunshine is sprinkling my face. I hear that little kid laughing again and a woman with red hair is smiling up at me, her eyes full of love.

But then the dream shifts. Something's wrong.

Pigface is here.

He's a silhouette that slips across the walls and ceilings, sliding long and tall and then short and wide. The shape morphs and becomes huge on the wall, covering it in darkness. Something glints and I see a knife.

Then a hand closes over my mouth. I wake up and open my eyes wide in shock. He's really here. And he's come to get me.

Chapter 10

revealer

'Come on, Cal,' he says and slaps my cheek lightly. But it's not Pigface. It's Beardy.

I immediately struggle and try to throw him off, but he touches a small piece of paper under my nose and my limbs go feathery light. I can't speak or move anything but I'm yelling inside. He drags me into an upright position.

Another nurse I vaguely recognise comes in with a laundry trolley. Between them, they crumple me awkwardly inside it and cover me with sheets. It smells of sweat and something rotten in here. I feel vibrations through the bottom of the trolley. I'm moving. There's a metallic clanging sound and everything rumbles. Sounds like an engine. I must be in the back of a van or lorry. 'Let me out! Let me out!' The shouts are inside my own mind. My lips are numb, and so is every other part of me. No one can hear me. Whatever was on that paper has immobilised me, just as if I were tied up.

After a few minutes though, painful pins and needles jab like knives into my arms and legs. The feeling's slowly coming back into limbs. Soon I'm able to haul myself out of the trolley. I land with a painful crash onto a metal floor. It's dark but I can make out that I'm in some kind of van. I crawl towards what should be the driver's end and bang on the wall, yelling until I'm hoarse and my knuckles ache, but no one responds.

I curl up on the floor, arms around my legs, watching the doors. As soon as the van stops I'm going to be ready for them. A couple of times I roll back and lift both my legs in a position ready to strike but we're obviously just at traffic lights because we soon move on again.

After a lifetime, I feel the van go over bumpy ground and come to a stop, then hear the doors opening at the front. There are urgent voices.

I get right behind the doors and wait . . .

There's a clunk of someone turning the handle and, as a sliver of light dazzles me, I kick the door with both legs as hard as I can. I hear a crunch and a high cry of pain and I'm straight out of the doors. Before I know it, two strong pairs of arms take hold of me. I'm outnumbered.

Beardy is bending forwards, holding his nose. There are bright drops of blood falling between his fingers onto the wet earth. He looks up, eyes full of fury. The two men on either side of me start dragging me towards a pool of bright light coming from what looks like a low, long farmhouse.

A small woman in her twenties with short black hair is at the door.

'Easy now, Cal,' she says. 'It's OK, you're safe.'

I try to wrench myself free of the two blokes holding me but their grip is firm. I twist to look at them. One is black and heavily muscled with his hair in cornrows and a tiny earring glinting in his ear lobe. He ignores me. The other is white with cropped dark hair. He gives what looks like an apologetic smile as he drags me inside.

I'm inside a country kitchen that should have homemade cake being cut by a jolly farmer's wife. Instead, a handful of people are standing around and looking at me. There's no Victoria sponge on the table. Instead, there's what looks like a couple of AK47 guns. A middle-aged woman with glasses and blond hair is standing in the middle of the room. Her face softens into a smile and she approaches me, then she gasps as Beardy comes into the room holding a blood-sodden hankie over his face. He mumbles something and disappears through another door, throwing death beams at me with his eyes.

The blond woman looks to the men with a questioning eyebrow.

The dark-haired one who smiled shrugs. 'The boy was a bit too keen to get out. Nathan copped it in the face.' He crosses his arms and his lips twitch as though he's trying not to laugh. 'He'll be all right, he's a big boy.'

'What the hell is going on?' I'm standing with my hands balled into fists. I could quite easily break someone else's nose at this precise moment.

'Please sit,' says the woman, gesturing to one of the chairs.

I slam it hard against the table instead. 'Just tell me where I am!' I shout. 'Who are you?!'

The woman raises her hands like I'm a dangerous animal. 'You're right to be upset, Cal, I completely understand,' she says. 'The last few days must have been deeply unsettling for you. But you're safe. For now, at least.' She pulls out the nearest chair and sits down, folding her hands on the table. 'My name is Helen Bonaparte,' she continues. 'My colleagues and I belong to an organisation called Torch and we have been trying to get into the Facility for some time to get you out. It has taken months of our people working there covertly to organise your escape today. And it wasn't a moment too soon.'

I find myself sliding into a chair, despite still wanting to run away. 'Look, just start speaking English because I don't know what you're going on about.'

Helen Bonaparte sits back in her chair, studying me. 'What did they tell you about the coma state you were in, Cal?'

'They told me I'd been there for twelve years,' I say slowly. 'That there was an accident when I was little.' I swallow. 'And that there was a boy who donated . . . tissue.'

She nods. 'That's all true. But did they tell you that they kept you in that coma? Deliberately? And basically stole twelve years of your life? And did they explain why you were given that donated brain tissue?'

I catch my breath. There's a dull pounding in my chest

that vibrates right up to my ears. I don't know where all the words have gone because I can't seem to find any to say right now.

Helen leans forward and clasps her hands in front of her. Her voice is gentle when she speaks again. 'None of this is easy to hear. I'm sorry. But they did something to you, Cal. Something wrong. They inserted a chip into your brain, entirely for their own purposes'.

I can't do anything but stare numbly. I sniff hard and swipe my eyes with my arm. 'I don't believe you,' I say in a shaky voice. 'That's sick. I think you're sick.'

Helen sighs. 'I think we're going to have to show you what this is all about. It's the only way. I'm sorry, Cal. This is going to be a bit distressing.' She nods to a man in a baseball hat standing by the sink.

He reaches for a long white tube and unrolls it. I realise it's a screen, a computer screen that's as thin and soft as paper. I don't have time to be impressed because he spreads it out on the table and the next moment I see an image of a room in the Facility – my room. Cavendish and some other people are standing around watching something and the view pans to take in the pod. I'm in it, eyes closed and I flush hot because I'm moving around like I'm walking along with my hands in my pockets. Thank God I'm not starkers. The camera pans round to show a computer screen just next to the pod. It's on top of a black box with blinking lights that the people are monitoring closely. There are pictures moving across the screen and I can see them perfectly. But they don't make any sense.

'Hang on,' I say, 'that's —'

I'm watching an image of the house on the hill. There's the hated shed and the old car out the front. Then there's the school playground. A game of football is going on with Amil and other friends, who come in close, laughing. Amil's making a loser sign with his hand against his forehead. In the pod, I kick my foot out and then turn around with my arms in the air, like I've scored a goal.

Just as fast, the picture switches again to one of Miss Lovett, my art teacher. But she isn't teaching a lesson. Oh no. She's getting out of a bath, soap bubbles slipping down her naked body and she's blowing a kiss at me.

I slam my hand down on the paper, face on fire, and the whole image disappears instantly.

'What was THAT?'

Helen Bonaparte moves towards me, but I step back. If she touches me, I'll kill her. I'm buzzing all over with shame and confusion.

'That was a secret film taken inside the Facility,' she says quietly. 'It showed you inside the suspension pod and it showed why you were in there. It's what that place is all about. They implanted something into your brain that allowed them to view your thoughts when you were inside that suspension pod. It's known as a Revealer Chip. The full name of the programme is the Cerebral Revealer Chip Study, CRCS or, as it's nicknamed, The Cracks Programme.' She looks down for a moment and I see her swallow.

I'm still at 'they've implanted something in your brain'.

I get the urge to scratch my head violently and my hands twitch. Got to stay calm. 'Why?' I say, voice breaking. I will not freak out. I will not freak out. *Breathe, Cal, breathe* . . .

'Well,' says the woman slowly, 'it started as a way to help people with severe disabilities communicate by computer. It was important work to begin with. But they wanted to see how far they could go and you, unfortunately, were their human guinea pig. They are trying to recreate the programme for mass use by testing it on others but it hasn't . . . gone well.'

My stomach, already heaving, goes into an icy spasm. 'What do you mean?'

She swallows again. 'All cases so far have demonstrated severe mental distress and sometimes a total psychological breakdown. That's the rather cruel side of the nickname for the programme. As in "cracking up".'

I'm struggling to get air into my lungs now. I can't imagine how I've ever done this without thinking. Each breath must be heaved in and out with a huge effort. Dots dance in front of my eyes.

'Cal? Cal? Are you all right?'

I clench my fists so hard, my knuckles strain white in front of me on the table. 'Never been better.' My voice seems to come from the end of a long, long tunnel.

Someone puts a cup of tea in front of me and I take a huge slurp, scalding my tongue but grateful for the heat and the sugar. My body and mind react to the drink and I feel myself breathing properly but my hands won't stop shaking.

'But why?' I say when I trust myself to speak. 'What's

the point? So they could have a good laugh at what was knocking about inside my head?'

'No, I'm afraid it's rather more sinister than that,' says Bonaparte. 'You've been out of circulation for a long time,' she says. 'Everything is about control now.' She pauses. 'I'm afraid that's the reality of living in 2024.'

CHAPTER 11

lab rat

2024? *2024?*

I hear a weird groan and realise it has come out of my own mouth. I've finally lost the plot. One of us is definitely mad. It's the only explanation for the ridiculous thing I just heard her say. I goggle at her, goldfish-like, too shocked to speak.

She flicks a nervous look at the others. 'Oh dear,' she says. 'You must think it is still . . . what, 2012? 2013? I suppose you would.' She breathes out a long exhalation before speaking again. 'That's when you would have entered the Facility in the first place as a small child. Time was essentially suspended then for you. We realise, from having been able to observe you these months, that much of what was happening inside your brain was probably based on the donor boy's real memories. You must have been living his teenage years. I've no doubt that it all seemed entirely real to you.'

I lean forwards and rest my head on my hands, fingers in my hair. I feel hollowed out, like someone scooped out everything inside that makes me who I am. 'What about the boy?' I say shakily. 'Who was he?'

Bonaparte gives a helpless shrug. 'I'm so sorry, we don't have that information. Just that the Revealer Chip was created using brain tissue from a donor. They'd previously tried to create something of this nature with artificial materials but it failed. They realised that actual brain tissue was required. Not that this was straightforward. You would have been pumped full of drugs for the first few years so your body wasn't able to reject the foreign object inside you.' She leans forward, her eyes kind. 'What I'm trying to say is that we don't know anything about the boy's identity. Nor, I'm afraid, anything about where you came from. But we're working on that. We hope to find more information in time. I hope we can help you to adjust to all this,' she says softly. 'It's such a lot to absorb, but the important thing right now is to get you to safety. There was a brief window of opportunity to get you out of there when you woke. We have been looking for signs that you might have been emerging from the coma, and waiting for an opportunity to get you out.'

I stare silently at the table for several minutes. Everyone's watching me. I wish they'd stop. A picture comes into my head of a lab rat in a cage and I try to shake it away. That's all I was. An experiment.

'But what did they *want*?' I say finally. I know I sound

whiney but I don't much care. 'I still don't understand why. Why do all that?'

Helen sighs. 'It's all about quashing any resistance. The Securitat – that's the people in charge – are a ragtag collection of businessmen and army generals. They believe in stamping down on any opposition to their regime. They wanted to perfect the technology and then planned to roll it out first to all prisoners, to monitor their thoughts and behaviour. But we believe ultimately they want to chip the entire population. If people's thoughts are no longer private, the authorities can root out dissenters and frighten the rest into submission. They'll stop at nothing to control people.'

'Can you get it out? The thing in my brain?' I scratch my head like I can scratch it all away. I have to force myself to stop because I know it looks mad.

Helen speaks gently. 'No. I'm afraid not. But they can only access it when you're at the Facility. The important thing now is keeping you away from them and keeping you safe.'

The other nurse I recognise from the Facility comes back into the room. He has some blood on his shirt so I'm guessing he's been sorting Beardy out. I feel a bit bad for smashing his face in, but what did he expect?

'We've been working on getting you out for a while, Cal,' he says. 'I've been turning up the resistance pressure inside the pod so it would strengthen your muscles and get you fit.'

'Track training,' I whisper and they all just stare at me with sympathetic expressions. 'I thought I was track training.'

I want to punch the walls until my knuckles split. And then the feeling drains away and I slide back into a chair and put my face in my hands. I wish I could stop thinking as easily as stopping those images on the paper screen. The idea that people have been watching me, watching every private thought I've had up there in widescreen feels like I've been burned all over. My face actually throbs from the blazing blush I can't seem to stop. Every time I think about them watching me, watching my thoughts about Miss Lovett . . . All my dreams and fears . . .

I look up.

'They knew I was waking up, then? If they could see everything?'

'No, they didn't watch you all the time,' says the nurse. 'I think there were signs and they gave you more drugs, but it definitely came as a surprise to them. But they were up to something new, Cal. We don't know what, but they had some sort of bigger plan.'

'Like what?' I say.

'We don't know,' says Helen, shaking her head, 'but we don't believe they would ever have let you go. You were no good to them awake. They may well have been planning to keep you in that coma for, well . . . the rest of your natural life.'

I shake so violently then I have to press down on my knees with my hands.

Helen clears her throat. 'There's something else, Cal. We're about twenty miles away from the Facility but when they discover you're gone, they'll easily be able to track you down. They can't do that via the Revealer Chip – it wasn't designed for that. But there's another way they can trace you . . . and we need to remove that possibility.'

She reaches across the table and takes hold of my hand. I'm too bone tired from trying to take everything in to resist. Her hand is warm and soft. She turns mine over so my birthmark is showing.

She looks at it and traces it gently with her finger before turning to the blond man. She sighs. 'First generation, I'm afraid. Bigger than usual.'

'What?' I say. 'It's just a birthmark.'

'It's not a birthmark, I'm afraid,' says Helen. 'It's a satellite tracking device that can pinpoint your whereabouts at any given time. The technology has come on considerably since it was fitted but because you've been there so long, you have the very earliest type.' She pauses. 'They fitted it when you were small, before you got used to that grotesque pod, in case you went wandering off. I'm afraid we have to remove it before we go any further.'

She's looking searchingly into my eyes, as though she can find an answer there. Understanding plops into my stomach.

'*Remove it?* What . . . you think you're going to just cut it out? No way!'

'Cal, I'm sorry but there's really no alternative.' She nods her head almost imperceptibly and the two blokes grab hold of my arms.

'Let go!' I struggle and try to wrench free but they're both miles stronger than me and all I can do is wriggle sort of helplessly.

Helen winces and picks up a roll of plastic sheeting and

spreads it across the table. She goes to a bag on the floor and produces a small medical kit, which she brings to the table. Then she gets out a bottle of antiseptic and the biggest, meanest mother of a scalpel I've ever seen. Next she goes over to the sink where she wets her hands and starts scrubbing at them with soap and a small brush, before pulling on a pair of thin flesh-coloured gloves, giving them a snap as she does so.

'I'm very sorry about this,' she says. Her mouth is set. 'But it won't hurt, I promise.'

'NO!' I'm struggling like crazy and another bloke rushes over. He holds me around the chest so tightly I can hardly breathe. One of the men stretches my arm out on the table into a vice-like grip and pulls my sleeve but I won't turn my hand over. I'm all the while crying out, 'No! Stop! You can't do this!' No one takes any notice. Helen rubs some sort of icy cold cloth over my hand, which immediately goes limp and numb. She nods to one of the men. 'Hold his head away, I don't want him to see.'

I catch the smiley bloke's eye and he has the cheek to look upset. He says, 'I'm really sorry about this, mate,' and takes hold of my face gently. I shout, 'NO! You'll have to break my neck if you try to stop me!' and he looks at Helen, who nods once. It somehow seems important that I watch. Surely she won't really do it? 'There must be some other way. You can't just cut it out!'

'Cal, you're going to have to trust us. You've had too much to absorb in a short space of time and it's impossible for you to think clearly and know what's best for you right now. I'm very sorry, but what's best is this. I'll be very careful to avoid too much scarring.'

It's a good job my hand is numb because I don't know what I'd do with it if it wasn't. My other arm is still tightly gripped in a way that means I can't move in the chair. I look around the kitchen, thinking about how I can get away. Beardy, or Nathan as he seems to be called, comes back into the room. His nose looks terrible and his eyes are all puffy. Do I see something triumphant flick across his face as Helen picks up the scalpel? I'm glad it's not him holding it.

'Hang on!' I shout desperately, playing for time. 'Why did he stop me from leaving the Facility if you were going to get me out of there anyway?'

'It wasn't the right time,' he says, his voice thick and nasal. 'We didn't have everything in place. You could have completely blown it for us. You wouldn't have got ten metres away before they tracked you down and then security around you would have increased.'

I look down and Helen Bonaparte is actually *pressing the scalpel against my skin*. I can't feel it but I shudder anyway. It looks like a pen's drawing a thin line of bright red in an L-shape. I can only feel a slight tickling sensation as she gently tugs the skin to one side as a flap. The very worst part is a meaty smell and my stomach heaves but I can't stop looking. She reaches for a long, thin pair of tweezers and rummages about in the gory wound while my blood pools in scarlet streams down my wrist and onto the table.

Then she's holding a black metal oblong with the tweezers. 'There we are. I hope you believe me now and understand why this was necessary.'

I stare at the tracking device then glare at Helen, hating her for cutting me and being right.

'I'll be as quick as I can getting you stitched up,' she says as she pours a chemical over the wound. Then she gets out a tiny needle that's already threaded and begins stitching my hand as though doing some embroidery. The tip of her tongue pokes out the side of her mouth. Each tiny stitch seems to take hours.

The blokes holding me relax their grip and I suddenly see myself jumping to my feet and escaping. But I know that wound needs stitching and, anyway, where am I going to go? I'm too confused to know what to think about anything. I'm so tired, suddenly it feels like Pigface's weights have been attached to my limbs. My eyes are gritty and heavy and I keep blinking.

A lifetime later she's done. She sprays my hand with something that instantly dries into a shiny film before wrapping gauze around the wound and bandaging it up. The dressing goes high, up and over my wrist bone too.

'All done,' she says. She throws the gloves onto the bloodstained plastic on the table and goes to the sink, where she gets a glass of water. She puts a couple of pills and the water in front of me and nods again to the men, who let me go and stand back. I immediately jump to my feet and turn on one of them, shoving him hard in the chest. But he barely blinks. Humiliated and close to crying, I sit back down again with a thump.

'Easy now, Cal,' says Helen. 'That local anaesthetic will

wear off quite soon so it's very important that you take these painkillers every four hours. You've had a minor operation and it will be sore for some time. If there is the slightest discolouration or oozing from the wound, you must take these antibiotics, without fail.' She pulls out a tube of pills from her pocket. 'They're very precious and you must not lose them. This is very important. I've sprayed a powerful antiseptic on there but you must watch for infection. Peel back the bandage every couple of days and check, OK?'

She moves her head, her eyes earnest, to make sure I'm looking at her. I feel exhausted now. It's hard to follow everything she's telling me.

'Cal, I need to know that you're understanding this. You've been in the same environment for twelve years. Your body is going to have to adjust very quickly to the bacteria and viruses that most of us are used to. Coupled with this operation on your hand . . . well, those antibiotics could save your life. Especially nowadays. Only a few people have access to drugs like these.'

'OK, I get it,' I say, thickly, running my good hand under my snotty nose.

The other woman comes into the room holding a black and white cat. And not just any black and white cat – it's the one I saw in that other place. My old life. It was there when I walked to Riley Hall, just before I woke up.

She's nuzzling it under her chin with a blissed out expression and Helen gives a tight smile.

'You can't keep that cat, Julia.'

The woman hugs the cat tighter. 'I know, but I wish I could.'

'I know that cat,' I say.

Helen gestures to Julia to bring it over. 'I'm not surprised. This cat belongs to Cavendish. He lives on site and the cat is allowed to go anywhere. But it has an important job to do now.'

'Job? What job? Don't hurt it!'

'I'm not going to hurt it,' says Helen patiently. 'It's just going to help put them off the scent for a while, that's all.' She pulls a small collar with a tiny leather compartment sewn into the side of it out of her pocket and picks up the tracking device from the table, which has been washed free of my blood. It only just fits into the compartment and she has difficulty closing the top.

The cat hisses and tries to struggle free but Helen quickly puts on the collar around its neck.

'Almost got it, almost . . . there.' The cat jumps out of her arms and pads to a corner of the room where it watches us resentfully.

'How long before they find out they're not tracking Cal?' says Julia.

Helen frowns. 'Not long enough. You three need to get going. The rest of us will go the other way and take the cat to the moors. It will buy some time, but they'll be employing all their resources to find Cal. They won't want to lose their precious research.'

I take a sharp intake of breath. Her eyes flick back to me and soften.

'I'm sorry, but that's what you are to them. That's why we had to get you out.' She claps her hands. 'Let's go, everyone. Now, please.'

Beardy – Nathan – whatever he's really called, eyes me again. I'm guessing I'm not his favourite person in the world right now.

But he's only got a busted nose. My whole world has been destroyed.

CHAPTER 13

someone else's memories

There's lots of movement and conversation as they prepare to go. Helen's speaking to me. I think she's going on about the antibiotics again. But there's a weird buzzing in my brain and I can only see her mouth moving.

I grunt and turn away.

They all go outside for a minute, leaving me alone in the kitchen. I rub my one free palm on my trousers, because it's sweaty. I can't stop shaking all over. I look around the huge kitchen to try to distract myself from all the feelings that are crowding in on me. Fear. Sadness. Anger. There's plenty of anger. I clench my one good fist and bang it on the table.

I sweep my eyes broodily around the kitchen and something snags my attention. There's a wooden dish rack attached to the wall and next to it a shelf holding neat rows of colourful spices in small glass jars. A feeling from my old life tugs at me, like an itch I can't reach. I frown, trying to understand it.

And then it comes.

Amil's kitchen. His mum has those same bottles, except hers are all jumbled messily along the back of the kitchen counter. A powerful memory of being warm and safe floods through me. I can almost smell yummy chicken curry and hear the chatter and telly sounds from next door. Then reality hits with the force of a punch and the room lurches sideways.

I've never really been in that kitchen.

Amil was someone else's best friend.

These are someone else's memories.

But it felt so *real.*

The whole thing is sick. I'm breathing hard like I've been running. A headache throbs with a regular beat over one eye. I touch my forehead. How did they do it? Get into my brain, I mean? I gently feel about in my hair to see if there is a scar but can't feel anything at all. I get a sudden image of Cavendish holding a rusty old saw from Des's shed and looming over me in a bloodstained apron.

My stomach flips over and the room spins sickeningly fast. I grip the table, hard, like I'm going to pitch forward into some sort of black hole otherwise. I touch my scalp again with the other hand. My head feels vulnerable, my skull eggshell-thin, like it could crack open and everything inside could spill out.

I'm not even sure what's real any more. Maybe I'm going to wake up again and find all this was some sort of horrible nightmare and I'm back in my old bedroom. Or maybe I'm still suspended in that pod, while people prod and probe . . .

Something is squeezing my chest like a vice and the walls pulse and shrink. I can't remember how to breathe normally. Little panting sounds are coming from my own mouth but they sound really far away too.

'Cal? Cal, are you OK?'

That bloke who smiled is kneeling in front of me. His hand is on my arm and I shrug it off like it burns. Everything is too loud, too bright. I want to go back. I don't want to be here. I want to climb back into my old life with Mum and yes, even Des and Ryan. My chest hurts. The edges of everything are shadowy but little fireworks are going off too. Sharp pins and needles jab my fingers and my hands are going numb now. Can't seem to drag breaths in and out. Dizzy. Can't breathe. Can't breathe! I'm going to die . . .

'Take this, quickly. Come on, mate, you're OK.'

Tom's holding a paper bag. He tells me to put it over my nose and mouth. I take it with trembling hands and do what he says, too scared to care about how stupid I look.

'That's it, just breathe slowly. In . . . and out . . . in . . . and out.'

Somehow, after a few minutes I feel better. The clattering inside my chest slows down and the world comes into proper focus. I can breathe properly again.

I mumble my thanks.

'No problem,' he says gently. 'Felt like you couldn't breathe? Like you were going to die, right?'

I nod, frowning. How did he know?

He smiles. 'It was just a panic attack. A bit too much carbon dioxide flooding through your body, that's all. Breathing into the bag redresses the balance. You're OK now. It's no wonder you're feeling a bit strange. I don't know how anyone could handle what you've had to deal with in the last few days without feeling a bit wobbly.'

I hand him the crumpled, damp paper bag. I don't really know what to say so I say nothing.

Nathan comes striding into the room then, still dabbing at his nose with a balled up tissue.

'What's going on?' he says sharply.

Tom looks up. 'Nothing,' he says easily, getting to his feet. 'Everything's fine, Nathan. How's the nose?' His face is expressionless but as his eyes meet mine I think something mischievous twinkles in them.

'It's really quite uncomfortable, since you ask,' says Nathan stiffly and starts looking in one of the kitchen cupboards.

Tom turns to me and pretends to rub his fists into his eyes like a toddler. He makes a silly face and mouths 'boo-hoo' silently.

A laugh surges up inside, surprising me. Beardy looks up and I turn it into a cough.

Tom checks his watch. 'Right, it's just gone six,' he says, all business-like now. 'We'll stay here for a few hours until we hear everything's gone to plan and then get on the road. Anything good in there?' he says, turning his attention to Nathan who is still rummaging through the cupboards with a miserable expression.

'No,' he says bluntly.

Tom goes over and has a look. 'Oh I wouldn't say that.' He turns to me with a grin. 'You, my friend, are in for a treat. It's time for Tom's baked bean and tuna hotpot.' He rubs his hands together. 'Trust me, it's not an experience you'll forget in a hurry.'

I smile, despite myself. He's nice. Funny. And he was kind to me back there when I was freaking out all over the place.

But I still don't know if I can really trust him.

I don't want to be around other people at the moment. 'Is there a bathroom?' I ask, getting up.

Nathan is leaning against the kitchen surface, texting. He ignores me.

'First on the left upstairs,' says Tom, tipping a can of something unidentifiable into a saucepan.

I start to walk out of the room.

'Cal?' Tom calls. He's frowning.

'Yeah?'

'You OK?'

I nod once and leave the room.

But I'm not OK.

I'm about as far from OK as it's possible to be.

I get into the bathroom and lock the door. I look in the mirror on the cabinet, just as I did a couple of days ago in the Facility. My world has been blown apart all over again since then. Will it ever be normal? Has it ever been normal? I don't want to be this lab-rat boy with a computer chip in his head. I don't even want to be in 2024. I just want to be back in my own life, mucking about and laughing in Amil's kitchen. But I know that'll never happen again. Never happened in the first place. There's only here. Now.

I lean in and examine my reflection. My face is pale, apart from the grey racoon rings around my eyes. I fill the basin with cold water and plunge my head into it. The shock makes my innards shrivel but I'm hoping it will help me get it together a little.

I dry my face on a hand towel that smells of washing powder and ordinary, normal things. My hair's sticking up and I push it back tentatively from my forehead. I lean in even closer.

It's there. I can see it.

A silvery-white scar along my hairline. The image of them cutting me open floods into my mind again. I drop my hair back and stand away from the mirror, heart banging. I can't pretend it's not real now. The evidence that they were inside my brain is right there, etched into my skin forever.

I close the toilet seat and sit down. My mouth floods with spit and my stomach heaves. I just focus on breathing slowly for a while.

They messed with my brain. They filled my head with memories that aren't mine. They looked in there whenever they wanted, like it was some sort of open room.

I can't handle it. But I have to.

If what Helen Bonaparte says is true, they can only access the Revealer Chip when I'm in that pod. And I'm not there now. Maybe I can trust Torch to help keep me safe. I think about my plan to go to Brinkley Cross and find

Amil and his family. Torch might help me do that. It's not much of a plan. But it's the only one I have right now.

I sit up a bit straighter. One thing's for sure. I'm never going back into the Facility again. They can kill me if they want. But they're not getting to that Revealer.

Looks like I don't have a whole lot of choice about trusting these Torch people right now.

I head back downstairs. Tom's cooking and Nathan is looking out of the window. His face is still like thunder and when he sees me he gets up and then goes outside. I can see him through the small leaded window in the living room. He's smoking a cigarette and pacing up and down.

'Is laughing boy ever going to let it go?' I say and Tom looks up. Steam billows around him and his hair is sticking to his forehead. He blows up from the side of his mouth but the hair doesn't budge.

'Don't worry about it,' he says. 'You're not the problem.' He carries on cooking.

It feels like something unspoken is hanging in the air. Tom sighs and stops what he's doing to check the back door is properly closed before speaking again. 'He's just realised that today's . . . an anniversary of something. Something painful.'

I don't say anything. Tom goes over to look out of the window, checking Nathan is still outside. He returns to the cooker and carries on stirring. 'His younger brother was killed exactly two years ago today,' he says quietly. 'He was about your age. I hadn't realised earlier or I'd have been a bit more gentle on him. He's just a bit pompous sometimes and I can't stop myself from winding him up. But I should have realised.'

'Oh,' I say. A wave of guilt washes over me when I think about the van door hitting him. 'How? How was he killed?'

'Officially he died while *resisting arrest* during a demonstration,' says Tom. 'He wasn't even part of Torch. Just an engineering student trying to protest on the streets against the regime.' He sighs. 'That's the kind of people we're —' He stops abruptly as the back door flies open.

Nathan comes in smelling of cold air and fag smoke. He looks at us both suspiciously.

'Right!' says Tom in a too-loud voice, rubbing his hands together briskly. 'It's ready. Brace yourselves, lads, we're going in.'

It's not too bad, despite all his warnings, and I'm surprised to find myself finishing my plate. Tom brushes away my offer to help tidy up and he and Nathan carefully clear up any sign that we've been here. He tells me that the cottage is owned by Torch sympathisers who are away on holiday and have given permission for it to be used.

'Why do you have to be so careful, then?' I ask. 'If they said it was OK?'

Tom glances at me, his face serious. 'Because we don't want anyone else to know we were here. It would be bad for them if it was discovered that they'd harboured known fugitives.' He carries on cleaning up.

I gulp. That's what I am now. A fugitive.

And I don't know how far they'll go to get me back.

* * *

Tom gives me a backpack and tells me it holds some spare clothes and stuff. Most importantly, he hands me a pair of trainers. Black with white stripes. I quickly put them on and tie the laces with trembling fingers. I instantly feel a bit less vulnerable. I understand now why I wasn't given any back at the Facility. Who can run away, without shoes?

They do some final checks on the cottage and we go out to the van.

The air is cold and misty but smells sweet and good. I find myself pulling deep draughts of it into my lungs. It hits me that I haven't been properly outside for twelve years and I have to hold on to the side of the van.

'You all right?' says Tom with a worried frown.

'Yeah,' I grunt back.

'Hop in the front, then,' he says. I hear the click of the van's doors opening and he goes to check the cottage one more time. Nathan climbs into the back and the doors close with a soft thump.

I open the passenger door and then hesitate, looking around. There's a long driveway bordered by low hedges and white mist hangs in long, spooky fingers all around. I get a mad urge to leg it down the driveway, even though it looks creepy and uninviting.

The thing is, I still don't really know much about this Torch lot. My mind buzzes. Should I go with them? Or should I try to make it on my own?

I could do it. I could run right now . . .

A cool breeze ruffles my hair and I shiver. It's dark out

there though . . . and filled with stuff I don't understand yet. Could I really look after myself? If I go with them, they might at least help me find my family. And after all, they did get me away from the Facility . . . I look down at my bandaged hand. I haven't forgiven them for that yet, but I guess it had to be done to stop Cavendish from tracking me. An image of that stark room and the pod hanging down like some monstrous insect cocoon makes me shiver harder.

I don't have many options right now. I've got no mum or dad. No friends. I don't even know who I really am. A wave of sadness passes through me and I swallow hard, squeezing my one good fist so my nails dig into my palm.

Looks like I'm going to have to trust them, doesn't it?

I wrench open the door and climb into the van.

CHAPTER 13

in the forest

We drive in silence for a while. The headlights bore two pale holes into the darkness.

I'm just starting to get lulled by the rhythm of the van when Tom speaks. 'So, Cal,' he says, keeping his eyes on the road. 'Here's the deal. My cover story is that I'm a teacher on half-term holidays. You're my kid brother and I'm driving you to stay with our aunt and uncle because our mum and dad are working. You injured your arm in the science labs at school.'

'I did?' I say.

'Yes,' he says patiently. 'You did. Everyone has a small ID chip implanted on the inside of their wrist instead of ID papers now. Except you. There was no need to ID chip you, where you were. That's why Helen bandaged that area too. CATS scanners need to touch skin to work. They're unlikely to bother checking because they'd have to take the bandage off.'

'Right,' I say, not much clearer. 'What about you, though? What if you get scanned? Do they know you work for Torch?'

'Oh yes, they know,' says Tom, frowning at the road ahead. 'But I've had a false chip fitted into my arm. It wouldn't pass the newer scanners in the main cities, but if we keep to back roads, it should be enough to get through the more basic security technology at any road blocks we come up against.'

My weary brain struggles to take all this in.

'What about Bea— Nathan?' I say.

'Don't worry about him,' says Tom. 'The van has a hidden compartment in the back. We're banking on him not being found at all.' The words hang ominously in the air. 'OK,' Tom continues, 'so your name is Matt Spencer and I'm Patrick. We live in Westport, North Yorkshire. But hopefully we won't get stopped anyway. Cal? Still with me, mate?'

'Yeah, yeah. Spencer. Westport. Got it.'

Tom smiles. 'I'm not surprised you're tired after the day you've had,' he says. 'Why don't you try to sleep for a bit?'

'I'm all right,' I say. 'Not tired at all.'

This isn't exactly the truth. I am *completely* shot to pieces. But I also feel like I've drunk about seventeen Cokes. I'm shaky and wired and can't imagine I'll ever sleep again. My neck isn't doing a very good job of supporting my enormously heavy head at the moment though, so I pick up the rucksack and squish it against the window so at least I can lean against it.

No way I can sleep. Better to stay alert. Still not sure I can trust . . .

Something wet and cold is pressed against my face. I open eyes full of sand and realise I've done quite a lot of dribbling on the rucksack. Must have dropped off. The light is milky grey and raindrops trickle down the windscreen. Looks like it's morning but I don't know how long I've been asleep. The door of the van is open and we're no longer moving. Cigarette smoke wafts in. Must be in Loz's van. Oh God, does that mean we're going to Riley Hall again?

I sit up, panicky, in my seat and then it all starts to come back to me. Being in the Facility . . . getting sprung by Torch. It feels a bit like I've just plunged down a roller-coaster as the images come rushing into my mind. I look at my bandaged hand, which throbs with a dull, steady beat. I need to pee too. I'm about to open my door to get out when quiet, angry voices outside make me hesitate.

'It isn't the time or the place to discuss this!' Tom's voice is low and urgent. 'We're doing nothing without his permission, you know that! If he doesn't agree then that's the end of it.'

'You're not thinking this through properly, Tom!' Nathan's words come as an angry hiss. 'A deeper debrief is the only way to get the information we need. Damn it, this is too important to waste time on polite requests! What do you think he'll say? "Yes, go ahead, be my guest!" Of course he won't! Would you agree, in his position?'

'Keep your voice down for God's sake!' snaps Tom.

Nathan swears and I hear the pop of him sucking on his cigarette. It reminds me of Des, whose face pops straight into my mind. I scrunch my eyes for a second to make it go away. Tom is now murmuring so quietly I can't make out what he's saying.

'We'll see about that,' says Nathan clearly. There are footsteps.

I hear the back doors open and close with a clang. Looking through slitted eyes, I watch Tom climb back into the van. He peers at me but I stay still, head to one side like I'm asleep. The engine starts again and the car moves. I keep my eyes closed but my heart is thumping. Why were they fighting? And what did Nathan mean about a 'deeper debrief'? I don't like the sound of it, whatever it is.

I haven't really been told what it is they want from me yet. Do they have their own reasons for getting me out of that place? I make a quick decision to be on my guard. I'm not trusting anyone yet.

After a few minutes I do a fake waking up routine, with a big stretchy yawn thrown in for good measure. It feels important somehow that they don't know what I heard.

Tom looks away from the road and searches my face before half-smiling. 'How you doing, buddy?' he says.

I shrug.

Tom yawns widely and then catches my eye and grins.

I think about asking him to explain what I overheard but don't know how to bring it up. 'You haven't really told me where we're going yet,' I say instead.

He glances at me. 'No, you're right. Sorry, we should have

made that clear. We're driving to another Torch safe house. It's in the Cotswolds. You can rest there for a bit and get your head together. We can talk about the future once you've had time to adjust to all this.' He pauses and flashes a kind smile. 'It'll all be OK. We'll sort you out, don't worry.'

I stare ahead. We're driving through a forest that feels like a dense green tunnel. There are no other cars on the road.

I don't know what to think. I like Tom. He does seem to care what happens to me.

I sit up straighter in my seat. I'm all fidgety. It's like there are so many questions, all crowded in together, and I don't know which ones to pick out to ask. At this present moment, though, I have other concerns.

'Tom?' I say.

'Yeah?'

'I need to pee.'

'Ah, OK, no problem,' he says and presses a button on the dashboard.

'Comfort break,' he says, presumably to Nathan.

The van slows and stops in a lay-by. I climb down onto the ground, which is crunchy with bits of bark and twigs. The rain has stopped now and sunshine is pushing through the clouds, splashing brightness everywhere. I go off into the trees to do what I have to do, looking around me as I go. Weird . . . it's not like I was expecting 2024 to be all jet packs and skyscrapers, but I wasn't expecting a normal-looking forest either.

But then I realise it's amazing in a different way. I do a gentle spin, looking up at the tall pines above me and I get all filled up inside. The sharp smell of the trees mixed with the warm earth and the sunshine sprinkling my face feel so intense and I have to swallow deeply. I wipe my eyes and cough in what I hope is a manly way as I walk back to where Nathan and Tom are standing. Nathan is leaning against a tree, smoking again and frowning as usual. He looks exactly like you'd expect after spending several hours in the back of that van. Rumpled and sore. His face now sports a rainbow of bruises and I guiltily look away.

'All done?' says Tom. His tone is light but he's constantly scanning around us, checking we're alone. His eyes have grey shadows under them.

'Can I ask something?'

'Of course,' he says.

'What's with all the smells?'

He smiles, puzzled. 'What do you mean?'

'Everything . . . it all smells so strong.'

The two men exchange glances and then Nathan speaks. 'It's because you've been cooped up all that time,' he says a bit grudgingly. 'You haven't been able to experience the world properly. You lived in those four walls for all those years. What are you, fourteen? Fifteen?'

'Fourteen,' I say.

Something passes across his face. He surprises me by giving me a weak smile, but there's sadness in his eyes. 'Plenty of time to make up for it,' he says.

I think about his brother dying and feel a spasm of pity. Maybe I'm bringing back painful memories just by being a teenage kid.

'I'm . . .' I hesitate. 'I'm sorry about hurting you yesterday,' I say in a rush, looking at my shoes.

There's a pause. 'Don't worry about it,' he says at last.

Tom opens the driver's door and emerges, holding a bag. He checks his watch. 'I think we should take another five minutes and have something to eat.' He looks at me. 'How's the hand?'

'It's OK,' I say. Actually, it's just started hurting like crazy in the last few minutes, like someone has flipped a switch and is gradually notching up the pain. Whatever Helen gave me must be wearing off. It's almost a high-pitched whine that only I can hear; an angry mosquito in my ear.

'Well, it does hurt a bit, to be honest,' I admit.

Tom goes to the van and comes back with tablets. 'Swallow these and then eat something.'

I gulp the bitter tablets back with some lukewarm water from a plastic bottle.

We sit on a fallen-down tree and Tom produces tuna sandwiches and warm cans of Coke. I start wondering if 2024 is any different at all and then I remember I have a dirty great computer chip inside my brain that shows people my darkest, deepest secrets. I stuff in my sandwich to distract myself, barely pausing to swallow.

'Easy now,' says Tom, but I ignore him and stuff the remains of it down before giving a ripe and satisfied burp.

'Feel better for that?' he asks with a mischievous grin.

The painkillers are starting to dull the pain already and I'm feeling almost half decent. A smile tickles my mouth.

'Blinding, thanks,' I say.

Tom laughs and then he burps too, even louder than mine.

Nathan swoops his eyes disgustedly, which just makes Tom laugh harder. It's like Nathan is Dad and Tom is the cheeky teenager, even though there's probably only a few years between them.

'I think it's about time we —' sniffs Nathan.

But Tom, suddenly serious, cuts him off with a harsh, 'Shhh!', his finger to his mouth. There are two sides to him, I can see, and the professional one kicks in effortlessly.

Both men go absolutely still.

'I heard something,' murmurs Tom.

Then I hear it too.

CHAPTER 14

cats

A faint snapping of branches is coming from somewhere behind us.

Without saying another word, Nathan runs to the back of the van and I hear the clang of the doors slamming closed after he clambers inside. Tom grabs the evidence of our lunch and stuffs it into a carrier bag.

'Quickly, Cal, get in,' he says sharply.

The back of my neck prickles with anxiety. We clamber in and Tom starts the engine before I've even closed my door. The tyres screech as we pull away from the lay-by.

'What was it?' I say.

Tom checks the rear-view mirror. 'I'm not sure, but could be cats,' he says grimly.

Somehow I'm guessing this isn't the kind of moggies I'm familiar with.

I open my mouth to ask more and then something flashes in front of the car. Tom swears and we brake suddenly. I'm violently jerked forwards and the seatbelt bites into my shoulder. Something slams into my side window and I gasp, looking into the face of a young Indian man, his eyes bulging with terror and his face bloody and scratched. His clothes are ripped and purple bruises and small red scabs spot his arms.

He seems to mouth the word 'help' and tries to open my door but I hear Tom clunk the central locking.

I spin to look at him and see a hard set to his face.

'He needs our help!' I yell but Tom just pulls away in a screech of tyres. I look in the wing mirror and see a pack of dogs emerging from the bushes with several men in black uniforms. The man crouches in the road and the dogs set upon him like he's a juicy bone.

'Why didn't you help him?' I shout.

Tom stares stonily at the road ahead. 'I couldn't, Cal,' he says quietly. 'He was beyond help. We'd only have drawn attention to ourselves. It might have meant you being captured again. Do you understand?'

I nod, reluctantly. I'm shaking all over and can't get the image of the man's terrified face out of my head.

'Who are those people? Are they police?' I clench my good hand and try to breathe. The lunch I just bolted down feels like it might come right back up again.

'More powerful than the police,' says Tom. 'They're known as Counterinsurgency and Anti-Terrorism Squads, or CATS. It's difficult to monitor some rural areas, so they send in these CATS to sniff out terrorists. Or at least that's what they say. Really they like to bully and intimidate residents. Black and Asian residents usually get it worst.'

'Why?' I say and Tom gives a heavy sigh.

'Because the whole regime is based on a fear of terrorism. There are regular attacks in the major cities and no one knows for sure who's responsible. Torch thinks the regime is actually behind many of them. It's their reason for identity chipping and it's why they invented the Revealer Chip. It's all about control.'

I look ahead, the man's terrified face still superimposed on my retinas.

'Help.' That's what he was trying to say. And we just drove away and left him there. I don't know what they'll do to him. Maybe he'll be killed. Or maybe he's going to end up in the Facility. Deep in some rotten part of me, I'm relieved it's happening to him and not me.

We drive in silence for ages. The sky has clouded over again and a thin drizzle is falling now. The windscreen wipers swish and thump rhythmically.

After a while we reach a motorway that has about ten lanes each way. It makes me a bit nervy and my back prickles with sweat. Tom closes all the windows and I can hear the low hum of air-con.

We stop at a service station to fill the van with petrol. Tom's face is serious now. All the banter has gone. Nervousness ripples in my belly. It somehow felt safer when we were in the middle of nowhere. I can't help worrying that every car overtaking us is filled with CATS or whatever they're called, all hunting me down.

Coming off the motorway at last, the traffic slows and thickens, no longer moving easily. We're at the top of a giant hill and below us, Tom tells me, is Sheffield. But it's hard to make out buildings because the whole thing has a kind of yellow fog hanging over it.

'What's that?' I say.

'Just rush hour pollution,' says Tom. 'It's known as the miasma. Car use has gone off the scale because no one feels safe on public transport these days.'

I stare at him, confused.

'Terrorist attacks,' he says wearily, making air quotes with his fingers.

We crawl through the suburbs of the city. The houses look pretty much like any houses, although some of the better-tended gardens have all sorts of colourful plants splashed over them. They're a weird contrast to the toxic yellow air outside the car. I swivel in my seat to look at some massive palm trees taking over one front garden. They look weird. Sort of tropical.

'The one upside to climate change,' he says with a wry smile. 'We get a few exotic plants. Unfortunately, that also means exotic insects so, if you see any mozzies, make sure you kill them quickly. Malaria is a big problem here now, and there was an epidemic of dengue fever a couple of years ago.'

'What the hell is dengue fever?' I ask.

'Believe me,' says Tom grimly, 'you don't want to know.'

As we crawl through the streets I can't stop staring at the

strange plants. Someone in a black 4x4 alongside us mouths something and a black screen instantly covers the window.

Tom notices. 'Try not to draw attention to yourself, Cal,' he says sharply. I turn away, stung. 'People get jumpy about being stared at.'

We stop at traffic lights. And then an alien creature suddenly appears at the window next to me and I just about lose my entire skin in fright.

It's staring in at me, its long flesh-coloured snout flat at one end and dotted with tiny holes. Its eyes are black and round. Even more bizarrely, it seems to be wearing a suit. And riding a bike.

'*What is that?*' I point a shaking finger at the window. That's when I notice lots of other creatures with the same face.

Tom smiles. 'Don't freak out, it's only people wearing their miasma masks. They keep out the worst of the pollution. You only have to wear them during rush hour. Look in the glove compartment.'

I reach forward and open it up and see two slippery pinkish things pooled in the bottom. I pull one of them out. It's soft and light and only takes on its proper shape when I give it a shake.

'What is it made from?' I ask Tom.

'Skin,' he says, matter-of-factly.

I drop it in my lap like it's burning.

Tom gives another easy laugh. 'Don't worry, it hasn't been sliced off anyone! It's synthetically engineered.'

I slip the mask on and, with a sucking noise, it clings to

my face. It gives me the creeps so I quickly whip it off again.

'Why don't you stick it in your rucksack for now? I've got several.'

I stuff the mask into the front of my backpack. Maybe 2024 is a bit more different than I realised.

Tom's phone rings and he brings it to his ear, eyes on the rear-view mirror. 'Yup?' he says and then goes quiet, listening to the person on the other end. He glances sharply at me and his face colours. He's frowning and then he looks furious. 'No,' he says. 'This isn't —'

The other voice seems to cut him off. He swears and then slowly lowers the phone.

'So who was that?' I say.

There's a pause big enough to park a bus in before he speaks again. 'We have to make a detour into the city,' he says tightly.

'Where to?'

He pauses again. 'To the university,' he says. 'There's someone there who wants to meet you.'

'Oh yeah?' I say, suspicion spiking my guts. 'Who?'

Tom looks at me and his eyes are strange. 'It's nothing to worry about, Cal. We have someone there – someone on our side – who wants to . . . examine you.'

I don't know why I'm suddenly prickling all over. Maybe it's the way Tom is looking dead straight ahead now and gripping the steering wheel, even though we aren't moving.

'What do you mean *examine me*?' I say, slowly.

Tom gives a heavy sigh. 'Look, there's no need to freak

out about this, OK? But there's an expert at the university who works for Torch. He wants to carry out some tests – with your permission, naturally. Tests that may help us understand the Revealer Chip a bit better.'

'Tests? What tests?' It's possible that I'm shouting a bit now. I feel like sirens are going off in my ears and red traffic lights are flashing STOP STOP STOP in front of my eyes. It's that word . . . *tests*.

'Calm down, Cal!' says Tom loudly. 'It's nothing bad. A couple of brain scans at most. But you can say no. You don't have to do it.'

Brain scans, tests, brain scans, tests, chips in my brain . . . no, no . . .

'No! I won't do it! No one's going near my brain! Not after what they did to me at the Facility!'

Tom slaps the steering wheel. 'I knew it was too soon,' he mutters, 'I bloody told them . . .'

I've got that feeling again, that the walls are all pulsing and coming in at me. I can't breathe . . .

'Look,' says Tom desperately, 'it's only so we can properly understand what we're up against, Cal, that's all.'

'You're just using me!' Blood pounds inside my head and I'm panting. 'I heard you and Nathan talking about this before! You only got me out of there so I could be *your* lab rat instead!'

'Cal! It's not like that, buddy, I —'

'I'm *not* your *buddy*,' I shout and in one movement I've grabbed the backpack and pressed buttons on the car door, praying one of them is what I want it to be. I tumble out just as the traffic starts to move again but somehow I've managed to stay on my feet. Then I'm running. I can hear Tom shouting behind me. I run between houses and past shops and just keep going, changing direction and ducking down any alleys I see.

I don't know where I'm heading but I don't stop running until each breath feels like it's being ripped from my chest. My nose and throat are coated in something thick and bleachy smelling. I lean against a wall. Dots dance about in front of my eyes. Is this the miasma Tom talked about? I rummage for the mask in my rucksack. I find the slippery material and pull it over my head. The snout part snaps into position and it quickly moulds to my face again.

I instantly feel better, although I can hear my breath going in and out in a creepy way. Yellow tendrils of fog are snaking around my body, like it's alive and trying to feel me all over. I force myself to breathe slowly and not panic as images of wires wrapping themselves around me pulse inside my head.

I feel a stupid urge to cry too and my belly hurts just like I really have been kicked there. I liked Tom. Trusted him. I thought he cared about me but all he wants – all *they* want – is to poke about inside my head and turn me into their good little lab rat.

I jump as a couple walking a dog pass by but they don't look at me. The fact that even the dog was wearing a mask should be funny but it's too sick and strange for that. It does at least help calm me a little bit and I walk down the nearest alleyway and find myself in a square, with benches arranged around a fountain that's all covered in slimy green algae and black stains.

There's no one about and I go and sit on a bench, leaning forward to put my head in my hands until I remember the mask is in the way. I try to think about what to do next, despite the fear and confusion swirling in my head.

What can I do? Where can I go? Maybe I can find a way to get to Brinkley Cross? But I don't even know where it is.

I sigh in frustration and the sound echoes inside the mask.

My hand is throbbing now too. I'm wallowing in an Olympic-swimming-pool-sized vat of self-pity when I'm suddenly yanked back hard against the bench, a vice-like grip around my neck.

'Just keep your trap shut and I won't hurt you,' says a low voice in my ear.

CHAPTER 15

knife

A long-handled knife is centimetres from my throat. 'Get up slowly,' says the voice, and I obey, adrenaline throbbing in my belly.

'Now turn round.'

I'm looking at a black boy a couple of years older than me, with big, dark eyes and a baseball cap pulled low over his face. He also has a dirty white cloth tied around his nose and mouth and it ripples gently as he breathes.

'Give me the mask,' he says.

Trembling, I take off the mask and pass it over. He pulls it on and it instantly changes colour to match his skin. Fear is suddenly replaced by a rush of fury that he's taking away my air. If he didn't have that blade, I'd fight him for it, even though my hand is throbbing like a git and my chest feels like it's being squeezed by a boa constrictor. I've got nothing to lose. I'm not going to let myself be controlled by anyone. I pick up the rucksack and sling it over my shoulder, meeting his eye. I walk straight past him and he grabs my arm, raising the knife higher towards my face so I can see the blade glinting up close.

'What's in there?' he says, nodding at my rucksack.

'You can have the mask, but I'm keeping this,' I say in a bold voice. 'If you want to mess me up just for some socks and a toothbrush, that's up to you. But you'll have to kill me.'

As soon as the words are out of my mouth, I think about Mum, or whoever she was, saying, 'You don't do yourself any favours, Cal, you really don't.'

I stare into his dark brown eyes. My breath is coming hard and fast. I keep my face set, even though my heart is banging hard against my ribcage. My mouth has gone dry and in my mind's eye I see the knife flick up and into my stomach, unzipping my flesh. I swallow hard.

And then the boy's face creases up.

He's laughing!

Even more surprisingly, he raises his fist up in a gesture of friendship. Confused, I raise mine back and he touches his knuckles against mine. I don't know whether he's going to kill me or high five me next.

'Keep the bag,' he says, grinning. 'You look like you need it. What's your name?'

'It's, um, Matt,' I say reluctantly.

'Matt, my man, I'm Jax. Glad to make your acquaintance.' Then his mood seems to change. When he speaks again his voice is flat. 'Don't think you can judge me, right? This ain't what I'm really about.'

I just stare at him.

'I'll leave you to get back to your mummy and daddy,' he says with a throaty chuckle.

I don't reply.

The boy does a funny saluting thing and then ambles off in the opposite direction, across the square and out of sight.

Great. So now I've got no mask.

I breathe slowly, trying not to panic, and thinking how I can bodge together some sort of plan.

There are things I need. Money, for a start. And somewhere to sleep. I rub my damp face and then shock fizzes through me as I realise there's someone standing at the entrance to the alley.

It's a pretty middle-aged woman in a smart coat and scarf, smiling sweetly at me. She looks like the sort of mum everyone would want. Something flickers and crackles around her and she disappears and then reappears again. I move closer as the realisation seeps into me that she's some kind of 3D projection.

'Have you noticed anything unusual in your neighbourhood?' she asks in a nice, reasonable voice. It's so realistic and looks solid but when I reach out my hand, it passes straight through her. She is looking at me wherever I stand and the effect gives me the chills.

'Remember, you could be prosecuted if you withhold information that could be relevant to a terrorism investigation.' Her face is so pleasant and smiley, you'd think she was on an advert for washing powder. 'Let's work together to keep our country safe. Report anything suspicious to this hotline.' She recites a number and then with a fizz and a pop she's gone. For a moment I stand still, expecting something else to happen. But it's quiet. I look up and see a bunch of small cameras mounted high up on the wall. CCTV.

I don't know how far Cavendish will go to get me back. If he's the inventor of the Revealer Chip then he's probably got a lot of influence with this regime. I bet he has access to all sorts of surveillance technology. I glance at the CCTV cameras again, my palms prickling with sweat.

Maybe he's closing in on me right now.

I picture a huge net falling from the sky and trapping me . . .

I've got to get out of this place.

Have I done the right thing, running away from Torch? Did they want to help me after all? Are Tom and Nathan looking for me right now? I need a place to think. I decide to try to find a library or internet café, or whatever goddam thing they have in 2024. I can at least look up where Brinkley Cross is and try to make some sort of plan. Or maybe I should try to find a way to contact Torch . . .

I get walking, head down, thinking hard. The rain continues to fall in a steady drizzle and even though it's still morning, the street lights are starting to come on in fuzzy yellow halos. I see signs for the city centre and just keep walking past shops and houses. The few people I see are wearing miasma masks, and faces seem to loom out of the smog like disembodied heads. Before long I notice all the other clusters of CCTV cameras on every building. With everyone masked up and the air so thick and dirty, I wonder what the point is.

I come round a corner and am facing a patch of park with a few benches and a war memorial in the middle. There are moving billboards on the tall brown buildings and massive words are rolling across them, bright against the dirty air.

WATCH OUT FOR SUSPICIOUS PACKAGES and *HOW WELL DO YOU KNOW YOUR NEIGHBOURS? ALERT CITIZENS ARE SAFE CITIZENS* and *SIGN UP TO YOUR LOCAL CATS BRANCH TODAY.*

Over and over the words roll past. Suspicious packages. Dodgy neighbours. They're seriously paranoid in this place.

I rearrange the backpack on my shoulder and am about to cross the road when I see something that makes me freeze. I sidle up to a parked lorry, heart pounding, and hide behind it, peeking out.

It's the Torch van. I see Tom talking animatedly on his mobile. He paces up and down. He's clearly having an argument with someone by the way he waves his arms around. Then I watch him very slowly drop his arm. He's looking straight ahead. A man dressed completely in black leathers approaches him, holding a crash helmet. He walks slowly around the van and then roughly pushes Tom backwards against the side. The biker guy gets something from his pocket and holds it over Tom's right arm.

Then he walks around the van holding out the scanning thing, or whatever it is. I creep along the side of the railings until I'm close enough to listen. There's ivy and stuff growing there that tickles my nose but I keep my face close, watching through the thick green tangle of leaves.

'You'll find that all my papers are in order,' says Tom in a confident voice. He rubs his hands against his jeans and flexes his fists. 'Now, if you'll let me go, I'll be on my way.'

The bloke in leathers has thin blond hair over a balding scalp and he puts his face close into Tom's. 'Open the back of the van, please.'

Tom starts to object and the man, one of those CATS people I reckon, smacks him in the face so fast and so hard that I hear the sound like a whipcrack in the heavy air. Tom says nothing. The CATS bloke walks to the back of the van and takes a gun out of his belt. Taking aim, he shoots the lock with a horrible shriek of metal.

He's just about to open the doors when Tom leaps into driver's seat. The engine starts with an angry roar.

The CATS guy yells and shoots the wing mirror. Glass explodes everywhere but the van screeches off around the corner. He's shouting into his phone now and within seconds I hear a repetitive thumping beat above me. A helicopter looms out of nowhere. There's a burst of firepower, a bright flash that I see above the buildings in the next road. For the next few minutes all I hear is wailing sirens. I'm too stunned to move and shaking all over.

People are looking out of windows to see what's going on and after a while I slide out from my hiding place and walk at the back of a group of office workers who have come out for a gawp.

Around the corner, the van is up on the opposite pavement, smashed into a bollard that's lurching to one side. There are black swerve marks etched into the tarmac. The doors are wide open and I can see clouds of inky smoke billowing out. The van is riddled with bullet holes.

I stare numbly, unable to take in what I'm seeing. The air smells of scorched petrol and an excited huddle of people are starting to congregate. A handful of CATS people wave their arms and one shouts, 'Get them back! It's going to blow!' and shoots into the air. People scream and move away in a wave and I'm carried by the momentum of the crowd.

There's an ear-splitting *BOOM* and then a moment of complete stillness and quiet. People are screaming and shoving to get away. I push in the opposite direction back to the street. My insides turn to iced liquid when I see the van, which is now just a twisted hulk of blackened metal. I stumble away, sour sick rising up in my throat.

I walk fast, not knowing where I'm going, the sound of more wailing sirens filling the smoky air. Little bits of stuff are flying everywhere like grey confetti. I see what looks like an alley ahead and, once inside, throw up against the wall until there's nothing left in my stomach. I'm shaking so hard my knees nearly give way. The smoke clings to my lungs and I cough and retch for ages. Further down the alley, I find some bins and sink down between them, pulling my hood down low over my face and trying to breathe.

I still can't believe what I just witnessed.

The van . . . all blown to pieces.

Nathan and Tom must surely be dead. Could they have survived that? I can't see how . . .

Waves of guilt roll over me. It's my fault.

They died because of me.

They were looking for me, weren't they? If I hadn't run off, they'd still be alive.

I might as well have killed them with my own hands.

CHAPTER 16

nobody

I curl up, arms around my knees and head tucked in, as though I can make myself disappear completely. Guilt, loneliness and fear chug inside, mingling together in a toxic cocktail that burns my stomach like acid. Rain falls softly and runs down my face, mixing with tears.

Should I have trusted them? I don't honestly know. All I know is that they're dead and that going with them before would have been better than having no options at all.

I have nowhere to go. I have no home. No family or friends. I don't even have my own memories. Des's ugly face floats vividly into my mind saying, 'You're nobody.'

Looks as though he was right.

I sit there for ages, getting colder, stiffer and more miserable by the second. Then I hear a door opening down the alley. Looking carefully around the side of the bins I see a man coming down the alley carrying a bulging black sack, a dirty apron straining around his middle. He's unshaven and a cigarette bounces on his bottom lip as he sings tunelessly along to music drifting from the open door. I pull myself back into the shadows and he slings the bin bag into the industrial bin so I feel the metal vibrate against me. He goes back inside and the music cuts off.

I can't just sit here like a stray dog. I've got to do something.

Got to make a plan.

Think, Cal, think . . .

Amil's house pops into my mind again. It's so vivid and seems to tug something inside me. It's not just pictures. It's a feeling too. A warm feeling. Safe.

Like . . . home? But that doesn't make sense. The donor boy lived with Des and Tina and Pigface. I can't explain it.

But then something hits me and I go fizzy all over and have to get up.

What if I also come from Brinkley Cross? What if it was my home as well as his?

I've got to find a way to get there.

I glance around me. I don't even know where it is and I'm wanted by Cavendish and his people. But I've got to find a way . . . I can't start living this horrible new life until I know who I am.

I'm shaky and my arms and legs feel like they won't hold me. I need food. I rummage through the bag I was given back at the farmhouse. There are pants and socks, plus a few T-shirts and a pair of jeans. The clothes look normal but the material seems to pool into almost nothing in the bottom of the bag. I can't help feeling just a bit impressed, despite everything. At least there's something cool about 2024. That's when I realise the hoodie I'm wearing still feels dry inside, despite the miserable steady downpour that drums onto my scalp and shoulders.

The antibiotics and the painkillers are also in the bag and I look down at the now filthy bandage around my hand. I think about what Helen said, about the antibiotics being precious. Right on cue my hand starts to throb, as though thinking made it happen. Maybe shock was taking my mind off it before. There's a bottle of water and an energy bar at the bottom of the bag. I eat, drink and swallow the tablets, plus some painkillers to help me think. I'm about to put the slim tube of antibiotics back into the bag but some instinct makes me slide them into my trouser pocket instead. At least that way, if I lose the bag, I'll still have them.

That's when I remember I've lost the miasma mask. I swear quietly but with a lot of feeling. Luckily the air's better now. Rush hour must be over. I gather up my backpack and start to walk through the now quiet streets to try to get my bearings.

I see signs for the city centre but reckon it's too risky to go there. I don't know whether Cavendish has got people looking for me yet but it has to be safer to keep to the backstreets. I decide to walk until I find an internet café or library. It's not much of a plan but it's all I've got right now.

I keep my head down and avoid the gaze of anyone I pass, but it's not hard to remain anonymous. Everyone seems to keep their eyes lowered as they scurry down the street or dodge from building to car. It's like the air is infected with paranoia. I keep moving too, walking for hours around the edge of the city, never stopping long enough to let the fear that constantly churns inside take over. I pass from one suburb to the next without finding any public building that will help me. My eyes are gritty and my feet hurt so I rest for a while in a small park, stretching out on the grass behind a stone war memorial so I'm out of sight. I doze off, despite how uncomfortable it is, and when I wake it's late afternoon. I stretch my stiff body and then a distant siren gets me back on my feet. I go out through the back of the park and head towards an area with lots of high warehouses, thinking I will at least be out of sight if any CATS are patrolling.

There's no one around at all. The empty streets are lined with soggy piles of rubbish and studded with dog poo. It's eerie here. I look around, chills creeping up my neck that aren't just because I'm cold.

Then I hear this low droning sound, like a swarm of bees. I look around quickly to see where it's coming from but it feels as though it's everywhere and nowhere all at once. It's getting louder by the second. Something makes me look straight up then and my stomach plunges with shock as something black and small comes hurtling out of the sky. There's no time to run away before it's zipping around my head. I try to bat it away but it's too fast and swoops out of range.

I force myself to stand still so I can see what I'm up against. The thing hovers right in front of my face, making a series of soft whirring and clicking sounds like it's talking to itself.

It's a machine, I can see that now. It looks like a cross between a giant fly and a tiny helicopter. The whole thing could fit easily into my closed fist. Not that I'm touching it. There are round protrusions like eyes that open and close at a dizzying pace. It's some sort of surveillance thing, it must be. And now they've found me. I'm going nowhere without a fight. I spy a broken metal pipe lying on the scrubby grass next to me. I grab it and hold it in position, ready to whack the bug thing out of the air, but it suddenly swerves and buzzes away, back into the grey rain-sodden clouds above me.

I stand there like a lemon. The pipe in my wet hands slides to the ground.

'Hey, that's some trick.'

The voice makes me cry out in shock and I spin round to see that boy, Jax, leaning against a wall nearby. I reach down and grab the pipe again, hefting it against my hand to show him I mean business. I'm not being robbed again after the day I've just had.

'Don't be like that,' he says. 'I ain't gonna do anything.' He moves away from the wall and comes closer.

I take a step back.

'So how d'you do that, man?'

'Do what?' I say through clenched teeth, holding the

pipe a little closer to my body.

'Get rid of a buzz drone?'

I don't have a clue how to answer this question. I stare back at him.

'Never seen that before,' says Jax. 'Them things find you where you shouldn't be, they zap you and tie you up, nice and tight, ready for CATS to come get you.'

He's not going to let it go.

'It's like you're the invisible man or something.'

I swallow, thinking about the fact that I have no ID barcode on my arm. These must be the newer scanners Tom mentioned. Apparently they don't need skin contact. It must have thought I wasn't a human. I guess I don't officially exist.

'Maybe they're having an off night,' I say.

There's a silence and then Jax guffaws. 'Off night! You're funny.'

I haven't got the energy to waste on this. 'Look, if you're thinking about robbing me again, why don't you just have a go and we'll see what happens?'

Jax looks properly offended. 'I'm not gonna hurt you, man. Remember what I said earlier, I said this ain't —'

'— who you really are, I got it,' I say.

There's another pause and he grins so wide, it's impossible to resist the smile tugging at my own mouth.

'So why you still hanging around?' he says. 'Haven't you got some nice home to get to?'

I think quickly. 'I'm . . . lost. I'm trying to get to my uncle's house in a place called Brinkley Cross. D'you know it?'

Jax puts his head to one side and screws up one eye. 'Hmm, no. Never heard of it. It's not round here, anyway. I'd know if it was.'

I feel like someone just delivered a right hook to my belly and hear a sound escape my lips like a groan. What if it isn't real? What if the name is just something my comatose brain created? I feel sick. I'm sweating and I'm cold all over. It's all I have to go on. I don't have any other options. I feel like I'm hanging from a clifftop and someone is loosening my fingers one by one.

'You all right, man?' says Jax, peering at me a little closer. 'You look a bit funny.'

I don't reply. Then I get an idea. A tiny handful of something to grasp onto. 'What about the Cotswolds . . . ever hear of that place?' I know that's real, anyway. It's where Tom and Nathan were taking me.

Jax looks down, biting his lip. 'Nope, don't think so,' he says. 'What is this? Twenty questions?'

Looks like geography isn't Jax's strong suit. So there's still a good chance that Brinkley Cross is real.

'Look,' says Jax kindly then, 'I don't know what's going on with you but I do know this rain ain't letting up any tonight. You can come back to mine if you want. It's not much, but there's always floor space.'

I study his face as the rain drips down mine, creeping under my collar and trickling miserably down my skin. I wish someone else could help me decide what to do. It's all so hard. It feels like every choice I make could lead somewhere dangerous and scary.

I could say no. I could just walk away and try to find somewhere to shelter for the night. I look around at the hazy yellow glow of the streetlights, the tall warehouses crowding around me, and shiver. The rain's pelting down now and I'm in a world I don't know or understand yet.

Should I trust this guy? Could I trust someone who robbed me just a few hours ago? With a *knife*? What's to stop him trying to do it again and leaving me lying bleeding in the road? But some instinct is telling me he isn't violent deep down. I knew people in my old life who liked to hurt people because it made them happy and somehow, Jax doesn't seem like Des or Pigface. Anyway, I didn't trust Tom and Nathan and look what happened there. They're dead and I still don't know if I made a bad call. Maybe I should have just stayed with them and let them do their tests.

Whatever. Sooner or later, I'm going to have to trust someone. I drop the pipe, which falls with a clang to the pavement.

'Thanks,' I say. 'I will.'

Chapter 17

kyla

We walk for what feels like days, past tall, old buildings that must have been fancy once but are now crusted with black from the filthy air. My trainers are rubbing my heels and my hand is aching. I'm hungry and tired and it's a good job there's no one around to suggest putting me back into a coma because I might actually be tempted right now, just so I could lie down.

We follow a path between buildings down to a canal. It smells like bad drains times about a million. I try to breathe through my mouth but can taste it now too, thickly coating my tongue. I put my hand over my face, trying not to gag. Where is he taking me, anyway? It could be anywhere. I see myself lying on the muddy towpath, blood pouring from a stab wound. A powerful urge to run from him trembles through my legs and I stop walking for a second.

He turns and peers at me through the peak of his hood. He scrunches up his face and then gives a comically cheerful grin. 'You all right, man? Not flagging on me, are ya?'

I just shake my head and he makes a big thumbs up sign.

I reluctantly carry on. He's not acting like someone who wants to stab me. He seems OK. For an armed mugger, anyway.

We walk along in silence, at times flattening ourselves against the green, slimy wall to get across parts where the footpath is broken and tangled weeds have taken the space back. I hear the odd *plock* sound and wonder what kind of creature can live in that water. It's high, almost lapping over the top of the towpath, like all this rain is just filling up a giant bathtub. Vast old buildings loom up on the other side of the canal.

There are a few streetlamps working here and there but after a while they run out completely. Jax fiddles with his watch and a powerful light illuminates our way in a bright, white wedge. We trudge on. I stay close, slipping sometimes on the uneven path and trying to grab at handfuls of weeds or flat brick to stop myself from falling in the water.

After what feels like ten more years, we turn off the towpath. We're at the edge of a housing estate. It looks like something from the Blitz. Most of the ugly, square houses have smashed windows and the black holes look like empty eye sockets that are still somehow watching our every move. Something flashes across one in a rapid burst of movement and I find myself moving a bit closer to Jax as he follows some mental map through a warren of boarded up narrow lanes. A handful of houses have lights glowing inside and I hear the odd barking dog and crying baby as I follow Jax deeper into the estate.

Finally, Jax stops. 'Welcome to my humble abode,' he says. 'Only temporary, as I say. You might call it a dump, but it's home, innit?'

Then he actually *winks* at me. Who winks? No one winks. I'm finding it hard not to like this weird guy, despite the whole knifepoint robbery thing. I feel a slight loosening of something tight inside me.

Inside it's warm and smells of sweaty armpits, frying meat and damp.

There are lots of people around Jax's age and a bit older sitting about inside a surprisingly big room. Some are stretched out asleep on mismatched sofas that leak stuffing. Others are on beanbags, furiously texting or playing games on phones. A soldier in full combat gear suddenly runs at me, screaming, machine gun cocked and I nearly wet my pants until someone shouts, 'Oi, move out of the way!' and I realise it's just a huge 3D image from a video game, projected on the wall in front of me.

A few of the people murmur greetings to Jax and he touches knuckles with one or two but no one seems that curious about why I'm with him. It feels good not to be looked at. The knot between my shoulders relaxes the smallest little bit, despite how tired and sore I am.

We go over to a corner where I can see a pile of scrunched up material. Suddenly the whole thing judders and shakes with a coughing fit and a thin brown arm appears, followed by a great mass of afro hair. A girl about my age, her skin a greyish brown, hacks and splutters into her fist and then flops back, regarding Jax and me with large dark eyes.

'Kyla,' says Jax, 'meet my man, Matt. He's the person who gave me the mask to help make you better.'

I decide to let this version of events go. I smile cautiously at the girl but her eyes are glassy like she can't see me. Her breathing is shallow and she has red spots on her cheeks.

'This is Kyla,' says Jax quietly.

She ignores me and coughs again. It's a horrible, painful effort that must reach all the way to her toes.

'How you doing?' asks Jax.

The girl just shrugs weakly.

Jax reaches into the tatty canvas bag over his shoulder and produces a can of Coke. 'Here, drink this.'

She pulls the ring with difficulty then takes a long drink, burping delicately at the end. It's like the effort of all this is too much and she slumps back again, coughing. She gives a queenly wave of her hand and then curls up so only the top of her head is visible above the sleeping bag.

'What's wrong with her?' I ask quietly.

Jax glances at me before gently stroking the hair off her face. Her eyes droop and I can hear the rattle of her breathing as she goes back to sleep.

'Her chest is real bad,' he says quietly. 'Happens every winter but this time it's worse. She needs antibiotics but no one can get them now.'

We both look at the sleeping girl. It's a bit hard not to

notice how pretty she is, despite being ill. I feel guilty for even thinking that because another evil-sounding cough wracks her body then, like a punch to the stomach.

A low voice behind makes both me and Jax jump. 'This isn't a hospital. I don't want her dying on me here.'

Jax winces and turns to the bloke in his early twenties who has appeared next to us. His limp fair hair hangs across his face which has a scar that seems to cut his hook nose in two. He's huge – about six foot five – and he wears a long, greasy black coat that makes him look like a vulture.

Jax seems to shrink as he meets the beaky stare. 'She's not gonna die, Zander,' he says. 'I think she's a bit better today.'

All three of us look at the girl. Even I can tell that must be a lie and I've never met her before.

'I got some stuff for you, Zander,' says Jax eagerly and produces what looks like a plastic wallet of credit cards from his jeans pocket. He hands them over to the man who examines them expertly before they disappear inside his coat. 'That's good. At least one of you is pulling your weight.'

Then he flicks his gaze to me. 'And who's this?' he says, eyeing me up and down.

'Matt,' I say firmly, determined not to be intimidated, even though I can practically feel Jax trembling next to me.

'He's my friend,' says Jax. 'He hasn't got nowhere to sleep and I said he could stay here . . . just for tonight.'

Zander puts his hand into his pocket in a deliberate way and I see the material bulge.

'What's in the bag, Matt?' he says in a silky voice and I hold it out in front of me.

'Just some clothes. I've got no money. The police took my aunt away and I'm trying to get to my uncle's house. I haven't got anything. You can look.' I feel like I just made a long speech and swallow, trying not to take my eyes off his face.

He whips the bag out of my hand before I can say anything else and rummages through it, dropping clothes onto the floor.

Then somehow I'm hard against the wall and can't breathe. One of his hands is at my throat, while the other pats me all over. Somehow he misses the antibiotics that sit snugly against my leg. His face is close. His pupils are huge and his eye colour mismatched. One is almost golden like a cat's and the other is green.

'I told you I had no money,' I splutter as he releases me. I regret it straight away. He smiles in a way that reminds me of a snake about to strike with a poisonous bite.

'Yeah, you did,' he says. 'So you can get lost now.'

'I tell you, Zander, Matt's not going to bring any trouble,' says Jax. 'He's the invisible man.'

Zander's whole body stiffens. 'Invisible man?'

'He got buzz-droned earlier and it just left him alone,' says Jax. I'm trying to beam SHUT UP! at him in giant letters but my telepathy skills are obviously rubbish.

'It was like it couldn't read him or something,' he continues eagerly.

Zander is looking at me differently now. His eyes flick to my bandaged arm.

'How d'you do that?' he says.

'Dog bit me,' I say instantly.

He smiles, showing small pointed teeth, and for a moment I imagine him sinking them into the other arm.

'One night only,' he says quietly. 'There's no room for freeloaders here.'

I meet his gaze, trying to match the cold contempt in his eyes. 'No problem,' I say through gritted teeth. 'One night. Thanks.'

Zander stalks off and Jax lets out a breath beside me.

'Who's that charmer, then?' I say quietly.

'That's Zander,' says Jax in an equally low voice. 'He's kind of in charge here. We all work for him and he keeps us safe in return.'

I wonder what it's like to have Zander with his crazy eyes as your protector.

Jax must read this because he grimaces. 'Ain't so bad. Better than the streets.' He looks away.

CHAPTER 18

zander's test

Someone hands me a bowl of curry and I practically inhale it. People talk late into the night, most of the conversation about games I've never heard of or football stuff that seems too insane to be true. I swear someone says Crawley Town are top of the Premier league, but I reckon I might be delirious from everything that's happened.

My eyelids feel like they have weights attached. Jax hands me a musty blanket, which I take gratefully, even though I'm still damp from the rain, which I can hear hammering relentlessly outside. I try not to get too close to Kyla, but she's restless. I can feel the heat of her fever coming off her. I drop off and then wake with a start to find her thin arm lying across my chest. I lie there, frozen with embarrassment then get really distracted by her velvety skin. I gently move her arm back into a comfortable position. Jax is asleep on the other side of her and the voices are getting quieter, replaced by snores from around the room.

Then Kyla has a coughing fit that violently jerks her upright. Jax is instantly awake. He pats her shoulder and murmurs soothing words as her body convulses. Tears leak from the corners of her wide eyes and she flaps her hands, struggling to breathe. I go cold all over. Jax's face is tight and frightened. She's in a really bad way.

After a few more moments it passes and she collapses back, a thin sheen of sweat on her face. Her lips are dry and cracked-looking. She's wheezy but breathing again.

I lie there, eyes bolted open, having an epic wrestling match with my conscience.

Kyla needs antibiotics.

I have antibiotics.

I need antibiotics too.

But she might actually die. Quite soon, by the looks of it.

I look at my hand and tentatively pull back the bandage. It's a bit red and puffy round the edges. It hurts, but not too badly. It's not brilliant but let's face it, I have a bit of a knackered hand while she has knackered lungs. It's not really much of a contest.

I wriggle to get the tube of pills out of my pocket. Then I nudge Jax awake.

'Waar . . .?' he says grumpily.

'Got something for you. For Kyla, I mean.'

'Eh?'

I hand him the antibiotics and he sits up straight, cradling the tube like it's as delicate as an egg.

He reads the label and turns to me, eyes wide. 'Where d'you get these from?'

I hesitate. 'I can't tell you. But I think Kyla needs them more than me.'

Jax carries on staring at the pills. He doesn't thank me and I'm feeling a bit annoyed until I realise he doesn't know what to say. I carry on talking to fill the silence. 'I think you take them three times a day.'

Jax just nods and then gently wakes Kyla. She grumbles as Jax coaxes her to swallow two of the tablets with some flat Coke. She lies back down and so does Jax.

He grunts something.

'What?'

'Thanks, man,' says Jax. Within a couple of minutes, he's gently snoring.

The girl stirs in her sleep and turns towards me. She opens her eyes wide and then her eyelids flicker and she falls asleep again.

I lie there forever, trying to do the same. My thoughts keep jumping around like something wild trapped in a cage. I'm picturing the twisted, smoking remains of the van and imagining the bodies inside it, all burned up. I squeeze the heel of my hand hard into one eyeball, trying to blank out the picture, but it's no good. Now I'm seeing Des's face up close, spit flying. Then Cavendish with his cold smile, explaining terrible things as though they're normal and everyday. And then there's the boy. The brain tissue donor. The one who gave me my only memories. I keep trying not to think about him but he's always there, inside me. Closer even than a twin. I know how it felt to be him. I know everything about him and almost nothing about me.

Then I'm in Amil's house and his mum is talking in a quiet, low voice, comforting me. But she isn't Indian. She has long red hair and freckles . . . it's so nice here. I want to stay. But then someone else is prodding me, hard.

I wake up sharply. Zander is crouching over me and poking me in the ribs. 'Wake up,' he says. 'I've got a little job for you.' His hot breath smells of alcohol and onions. 'Get up.'

'What . . . now?' I say.

His eyes narrow. 'Yes, now. You stay here, you pay your way. Even for one night.' He touches his coat pocket meaningfully. Something pointed is in there. A gun, or maybe a knife. He blinks. 'You're mistaking this for a request. Get up.'

I carefully get to my feet, keeping my eyes on his.

'So you're the invisible man, according to Jaxon,' he says. 'Let's see how invisible you really are.'

He gestures with his hand in the pocket. We step around the bodies that are sighing, snoring and emitting puffs of bad breath. I'm breathing heavily, scared, but I don't want him to know that. He's a bully. He gets off on making people feel small inside so I stand tall even though my knees are trembling. He could be taking me anywhere. Again, I picture myself bleeding in a gutter. But he knows I have no cash so why bother?

I think about making a run for it all the same but, once outside, there's no real chance of me doing it. He looks like he could be fast, plus he's walking close enough for me to feel the bulge of his weapon in his coat pocket. His leather coat creaks gently as we move and his onion breath keeps coming in gusts against my face. 'Where are we going?' I say. I try to sound calm but my teeth are chattering.

'Not far. I've got a little test for you,' says Zander. 'This is your way of thanking me for my hospitality.'

I can't think what he could possibly want from me and panic lurches in my stomach. We walk through the empty streets for ages. Zander moves in a silent prowl, dodging open spaces and sliding from building to building like a slippery shadow. I try to do what he does. Being with him is bad enough, but I don't want to get picked up by CATS either. I shiver involuntarily at the thought of them finding out that I escaped from the Facility. Better see what he wants and try not to freak out.

We retrace our steps along the canal and then go a different direction so that after about five minutes we're amongst what looks like tall office blocks. After a while we come to a smart-looking plaza. Glass buildings rear up on all sides, so tall I get neck-ache looking up. Zander pulls me back into the shadows. I feel something press against my shoulder blades and there's a soft, deadly click.

'Now then, here's what you're going to do,' he whispers. 'You're going to walk across that square and I'm going to see if you're as invisible as Jax says you are.'

'That all?' I say. 'Just walk?'

'The whole square is spiked with security lasers,' he says. 'They can only be set off by humans. Foxes were causing too many false alarms. So the cameras and alarm systems only kick in when they sense ID chips. And you and I both know that you aren't chipped, don't we, Matt?'

'I don't know what you mean,' I say pathetically and Zander digs the gun in harder.

'Don't mess with me,' he hisses in my ear. 'Now go.'

He shoves me hard and I cry out and stumble into the brightly lit square.

I stand rooted to the spot. I'm breathing hard. I'm scared to move a muscle in case alarms start screeching all around and men in balaclavas appear from the sky on ropes. But two, three, four seconds pass and nothing happens. He said they only get activated by ID chips, didn't he? And there wouldn't be any point bringing me here otherwise. Would there? Well, then . . . but I'm still frozen.

'Oi!' hisses Zander and cocks his head to indicate I should move. He waves the gun at me.

I take a deep and shaky breath of the cold night air. The rain has stopped but the wet marble flooring gleams like black silk around me. I slide my right foot forward and pause, heart crashing against my ribcage and cold sweat trickling from my armpits inside my clothes. Nothing happens so I slowly move the other foot forward.

Nothing. No men on ropes. No *wah-wah-wah* of sirens.

I take a few tentative steps, sliding my feet on the slippery ground as though lifting them to walk properly will somehow jinx everything.

A couple more steps . . .

I realise I've been holding my breath and I let it out in a

rush. I think it's going to be OK . . .

And then everything changes.

Terror clutches at my insides as a bluey-white light suddenly appears as a long column in front of me. It silently creeps up and over my body. I look up for its source and see its coming from a device high up on the side of the building. It crawls upwards and I close my eyes against the blinding brightness of it. Then it snaps off and is gone. I daren't move. I daren't breathe or blink or anything.

But nothing happens. I feel like laughing out loud with relief. I hear a soft repetitive sound and see that Zander is grinning broadly and gently clapping his hands together.

He gestures for me to move around a bit more. But I'm fed up with being a performing monkey for him. So I walk defiantly back to where he is leaning against the wall, a sly smile on his face.

'Excellent,' he says, grinning broadly. 'Now then, Matt. I've got a business proposition for you . . .'

As we walk back, Zander speaks, his breath making cloudy puffs in the chilly night air.

Here's his proposition: I hang around for a few weeks and help him with his 'work'. It doesn't take a genius to work out that this involves thieving. But he claims he has a 'foolproof system' and no one will get caught. He'll pay me a bit, but, here's the most interesting part, he'll not only get me some fake papers but reckons a mate of his can fit me with a false ID chip that passes routine checks.

'Why would you think I —?' I start to say, not sure I want him to see how much I might need this.

'Don't take me for an idiot,' he interrupts. It's like a shutter has slammed down on his new friendliness. His eyes glint, cold and hard. 'I heard what Jaxon said, about you being "invisible". I know you're not chipped. I don't much care why. But you know it and I know it too.'

I look at my feet. He's right. I was mad to think I could get to Brinkley Cross on my own. How long before I get spotted and picked up? I'd still have to be careful about being seen on regular CCTV but at least this way I'd have papers to check if I get stopped by CATS. Maybe I could get myself back on my feet a bit; learn a little about this strange world I've woken up to. And then I can try to find out where home is.

It's seriously tempting.

'I've got a question before I agree to anything.' I say.

Zander stops abruptly next to me and looks questioningly into my face.

'Have you heard of somewhere called Brinkley Cross?'

'What?' His irritated voice is taut as a wire. A muscle in his cheek twitches and his eyes are cold. There's a sweetish, musty smell rising from his coat, although I probably don't smell that great either right now.

I repeat the question.

'Why you asking me about this now?' he says. 'I'm trying to strike a deal with you here.'

'I know,' I say, swallowing, 'but I need to know something important before I agree to anything.' I meet his glare and make myself not waver or blink. 'Brinkley Cross. Can you look it up or something?'

He swears quietly and gets out his phone, then points it at the nearest wall. A crystal clear projection the size of a computer screen appears on the wall with a slightly different Google logo than the one I know. Despite everything that's happening, the normal part of my brain itches for a phone like that too. He mumbles 'Brinkley Cross' grudgingly. A 3D map instantly appears. It shows a satellite image of a town. According to the sidebar it's just fifty miles north on the motorway from here.

My knees almost give way.

It's a real place! I didn't dream it. I want to laugh and punch the air and do a silly dance all at once. It's not much to go on but it's something! I feel like it's calling me, pulling me back. I have to get to Amil's place. They have some connection with my real life, I know it. If not, then they'll help me, I'm sure. Maybe there's even a family waiting for me there. But first I need money and fake ID.

I hold out my hand to shake.

'I'll do it,' I say, 'but two weeks only. I've got somewhere I need to be.'

Zander grins slowly, his wolfish teeth glinting in the darkness. He takes my hand and shakes it hard.

Chapter 19

maestro at work

I'm sure it's five minutes later when someone is shaking me awake. I feel like I've been hit all over with a baseball bat. I groan and try to focus on who's next to me. It's Jax, leaning in a bit too close and looking annoyingly well rested. His big brown eyes are centimetres from mine.

'Come on,' he says, 'got you this.' He puts down a cup of tea in a cracked, stained mug next to me. 'Zander says I'm to show you the ropes.' He sits back on his haunches and watches me as I sit up and take a grateful slurp of the hot, sweet drink. Kyla is fast asleep next to me, her breathing a bit noisy but steady in rhythm. Jax reaches down and tenderly pulls her sleeping bag up a little higher, tucking it under her chin. He catches me watching, and blinks, then looks away and gets to his feet.

'So, drink that, yeah? And we'll get started.'

I'm worrying a bit about what I've got myself into as I wash my face in the bathroom. The mirror is dappled all over with rust and black mould. The hand towel is soaking wet. Whatever colour it once was has long faded. I give it a sniff, grimace, and then drop it back where I found it. I use my sleeve to dry my face instead.

Lots of people are still sleeping as we leave the quiet house.

Outside it's grey and overcast. There's a smell of warm concrete, burned rubber and wee. The estate doesn't look much better in the daytime. The windows of most of the houses are smashed and some are streaky with black smoke damage. We only see two people – an old lady slowly carrying a bag of shopping, and a boy about my age who scurries into a house with his hood covering his face.

We get to the canal again and step down onto the crumbling path. It's wider than it seemed in the dark but the smell is just as bad and quickly coats the inside of my nose and throat with something stagnant and rotten. Huge warehouse-type buildings with broken windows loom on the other side of the water. We have to fight through nettles and thorny fingers of plants that reach across the path. The water looks even higher than it did before and slops over the towpath at certain points, soaking my trainers.

Jax is almost silent. He lopes along in front of me, all arms and big feet, head down. He's fast because of his long, skinny legs and I have to hurry to keep pace with him.

'So how long have you worked for Zander, then?' I say, hoping some conversation might help with the jangling nervous feeling in my belly that isn't just from the lack of breakfast.

He flicks a look back over his shoulder. 'Few years. Dunno,' he says and then stops abruptly. 'Look, I know what you think.' He turns to me. His dark eyes are serious. He swipes a hand across his chin.

'Uh . . . what do I think?' I say with a small laugh.

'That I'm nuts to be working for a creep like him?'

'I'm not thinking that,' I say feebly.

He swoops his eyes. 'Sure you ain't.'

We walk along in silence for a minute and then he stops abruptly. 'I do it so me and Kyla don't have to live on the streets, OK? I gotta look after her. I promised her mum.'

'OK!' I say, palms up. 'Jeez, I didn't even say anything!'

'No . . . well, that's all right, then,' he says grumpily and carries on walking, a bit slower now. 'You prob'ly have no idea what it's like for us. Expect you've always had a nice home and never had to look after yourself.'

I sigh. 'You have got *no* idea,' I mutter.

He just snorts in disbelief. He's completely different to how he was last night. Maybe he's planning to shop me. Maybe him and Zander are up to something between them. I look around, half wondering whether I should try to go right now and make it on my own.

We're at the end of the towpath and I can see large metal sheds that look like factories ahead. Jax mutters something under his breath.

Tiredness and irritation surge up inside me, forcing words out. 'Look, what's your problem, Jax?!' I say. 'You invited me back in the first place!'

He stops and we face each other, both breathing heavily, eyeballing each other. He makes a frustrated noise and his shoulders drop. 'I'm just . . . it's . . .' He runs his hands through his hair. 'What am I going to do if she dies, man?'

So that's it. This is really about Kyla. I think about what Zander said about kicking them out, and the horrible noises coming from her lungs last night. Any lingering doubt that I did the right thing in giving away the medicine fades. On cue though, my cut throbs and I give my hand a dismissive shake.

'The people who gave me that medicine,' I say, 'they said it was good stuff. Hard-to-get stuff. It should help her. She's not going to die. I'm sure she'll be OK.'

Jax gives a weak smile. 'You really think?'

I smile back. 'Yeah, I really do.'

It feels like the right thing to say.

Turning off the towpath, we come back into the place we met again last night, among factories and warehouses. Vans and lorries snake around the roads and there are a few people in overalls about the place but it's mainly quiet.

We go to a spot near the back and Jax explains why we're here.

Seems that most areas of the city don't have the sophisticated cameras on the outside like in the plaza that Zander took me to last night. They have them inside warehouses and factories but on the outside they have regular CCTV. Zander's gang has developed a method to moving around and staying below the radar. One of Zander's crew worked out that each camera operates on a cycle of, say, one minute on and one minute off. Some work for longer, some less. There have been electricity shortages and all sorts of power surge problems so this has been the only way the authorities can keep so many going at once. So when you're in built-up areas, you look to see how long a camera goes still for and then you can dodge them. That's why Jax was walking in that weird way last night when we were out in the open.

Some of the cameras are broken in this part of the estate, so it's a good place for Jax to show me the ropes, he explains.

'So go on,' he says, 'I want you to pretend those cameras there and there,' he gestures with his head, 'are on a cycle where the nearest one switches off after three seconds. Then you move and count to three for the next one. And again. And keep close to the shadows. See if you can get all the way across to the fence.' He pauses. 'Got it?'

'Er, I think so,' I say.

'Go on, then.'

It's a lot harder than it looks. I've only walked about a metre when Jax makes a noise like a loud klaxon and waves both his thumbs down.

'Fail!' he says happily. 'You walked right into the open there.'

I try again, this time pressing myself close to the walls, counting, then darting across to the next building. I look at Jax who is expressionless. Must be doing it right this time.

I repeat the process until I get to the next building and then the next. I get to the other side and turn round, flushed and triumphant. I really think I'm getting the knack of this.

But Jax starts slowly shaking his head.

'Matt, Matt, Matt,' he says, with a heavy sigh. 'They just got a clear shot of your ugly mug.'

Irritated, I have another go.

He makes the klaxon sound again. 'They already got you tied up in some cell,' he says. He screws up his eye, as though listening to something. 'I think you're being beaten up by a big, bald guy called Skin about now.'

I glare back at him although a tiny part of me wants to laugh too. 'All right, genius,' I say. 'Why don't you show me how it's done, then?'

Jax wiggles his fingers and shunts his arms forward so the sleeves of his hoodie rise up, exposing his knobbly wrists. 'Prepare to watch a maestro at work,' he says and glides away from the wall.

All of his awkward gangliness seems to disappear when he's doing his stuff. He moves smoothly, darting and slinking along, almost like he's made of something fluid rather than flesh and blood.

I watch and concentrate as the seriousness of this takes hold. I have to get it right. If I mess up when Zander sends me out on a job, I'll get caught. And if I get caught, they'll take me back to the Facility. I swallow as an image of that pod swims in front of my eyes. My hand involuntarily goes to the scar on my head.

I can't – won't – allow that to happen.

'Right,' I say, 'Let's have another go.'

It's not perfect this time but it's better. I do it again and again and by the time Jax announces it's lunchtime, I can see a bit of grudging admiration in his eyes. He takes me to a dodgy-looking burger van on the edge of the estate. I'm so hungry I'd eat the polystyrene box the food comes in. I realise I have no money as Jax orders.

'Don't worry,' he says, glancing at me and reaching into his pocket. 'I trust you.'

I smile weakly. Trust me? He doesn't even know my real name.

Chapter 20

nothing to do with me

I learn quickly.

Jax and Zander teach me a whole range of skills I might have missed out on with a normal education. Not just about avoiding CCTV. Also how to climb through broken windows without getting sliced to bits. I learn about a whole range of digital alarm systems and the passcodes needed to disable them. He gives me a set of lock picks and I find myself pretty nifty with the old fashioned sort of lock too.

That's my job, circumventing the laser security and getting inside to turn it off, making it safe for the others. Zander has a team of eight, who he rotates. He teases Jax cruelly, saying he's clumsy and his big feet get in the way but he's obviously valuable to him because he's often included on the jobs we do. I like it best when Jax is there. We tease each other and joke about a bit. It feels good. Like I'm a normal kid, despite all evidence to the contrary. He never asks me questions, although sometimes I see him watching me. When I catch his eye he gives a big grin and cracks a joke but my guess is that he's wondering where I came from. But people in this house don't ask questions. Sometimes he stares into the distance and I wonder if he's picturing some other life too.

As for Kyla, the antibiotics do their stuff and after a couple of days she's able to get up. She looks frail and still coughs a bit but her eyes are brighter.

She does this stretching thing, standing on her toes like a dancer, moving her long neck from side to side. If she catches me staring, she smiles as though it's funny and I look away, cheeks burning. Because she's not strong enough yet to come on any jobs, she stays at the house while we work. She likes making cakes. Which would be great, but they're really terrible cakes – either so hard you're in danger of losing a tooth, or undercooked with craters in the top where they haven't risen. I eat them anyway. Jax teases her and she rolls her eyes a bit and clouts him round the back of the head with her hand.

I can't make out what the story is between her and Jax. He looks at her with puppy eyes quite a lot but I don't think she feels the same. Not that it matters to me. It's not like it's got anything to do with me.

One night, I'm walking back along the towpath at the end of the job. It's just me, Zander, Jax and two other guys in their early twenties. Zander doesn't like to park his car by the house so the car and the stolen goods get left in a lock-up at the city end of the canal. We always walk the last bit. Seems there was once a road into the estate but the canal flooded badly on one side and now this is the only way in. But it's a miserable journey and tonight it feels ten times harder.

The whole evening has been one big struggle. I'm tired and have a headache that nags above one eye. I'm cold and just want to get into my sleeping bag and pass out. We saw some CATS people earlier – lots of them – and Zander made a change of plan to move to another warehouse in a different part of the city. Worried thoughts jab at me as I picture manhunts and sniffer dogs all laid on by Cavendish just for me. Is it only a matter of time until I get picked up?

And do I really want to be thieving like this anyway? I don't like doing it. I'm worried about it becoming too easy. What then? Do I end up like Zander and the older ones of his gang? Sleeping with a weapon and never really trusting anyone? Having dead eyes that slide about and never really smiling? Never having a proper home or people who care about me?

All this grinds away inside and so I'm not concentrating when Jax calls out some warning to me. The next thing, my toe smashes into something hard and I trip. I'm falling sideways. I see the look of shock on Jax's face as I fly off the towpath. Then I slam into the filthy water. It instantly fills my mouth. I go under, gasping and choking. It's dark and cold and I thrash about. I can't swim! I'm being dragged down. I surface again and then go back under. Something has hold of my foot. My lungs are screaming, tearing, burning. I'm going to die! I'm going to die right here before I've even had a chance to live. Hurts my chest . . . can't breathe . . .

Lights start exploding inside my head.

And then I'm above the surface again and a long brown arm is around my neck, pulling me backwards, and then hauling me back onto the towpath.

Jax is dripping all over me. He leans over, gasping for breath. 'You all right, man? You OK? Matt!' He slaps my cheek gently, his eyes wide and scared.

I struggle to a sitting position and then throw up all over myself. I can taste that chemical water and I heave over and over again. I look up blearily to see Zander staring down at both of us, a look of distaste on his face and zero sympathy.

'If you two want to go for a swim then feel free. But I'm not standing around all night waiting for you.'

I wipe my mouth with a shaking hand and glare up at him. I open my mouth to bite back but Jax squeezes my shoulder warningly. 'You're OK, Matt, you're OK,' he says. 'Think that's enough excitement for one night, yeah? Come on.' He gets to his feet and holds out his hand. I take it and he helps haul me to my feet.

'Told you to watch out for those bricks, but did you listen?' He's smiling kindly.

'Thanks, Jax,' I say quietly and he just nods and claps me on the back.

'Forget about it,' he says. 'Owe you one, anyway. For Kyla,' he adds in a whisper.

CHAPTER 21

stewp

I sleep heavily that day, but have strange dreams where harsh voices mutter threats in my ears. I'm underwater and can see Cavendish's face floating just above the surface. I'll die if I stay under, but I'll die if I come out too. Then I'm looking at a brain floating in a glass jar and Cavendish is prodding it with a pencil, laughing.

I wake up suddenly. Sitting up, I groan. I don't know what was in that canal water but my guts feel terrible. The house seems empty and I wonder where everyone is as I pad through and take a shower – cold, because the heating only works when a guy called Mab manages to hack into some sort of power company database.

I'm shivering when I come back into the room with just a towel round my waist. I start as I see Kyla reading a tatty paperback on the sofa. She looks me up and down. I instantly turn into a red traffic light as I snatch up my clothes.

'Where is everyone?' I say in a strangled voice.

'Out on a job,' she says, with a small cough. 'Zander gave you a lie in. Said his golden boy deserved a rest.'

I flush even more. 'Don't call me that.'

Her face softens. 'OK,' she says quietly. 'Look, he didn't really. I heard you took a dip in the canal? You were muttering in your sleep. Sort of feverish. Zander thought you'd be a liability if you went.'

'Oh,' I say. I don't know how to put my next question but Kyla seems to guess it from my expression.

'Don't worry!' She smiles. 'You didn't tell us your deepest, darkest secrets or anything!'

I grunt and grab some clothes and a hoodie pinched from a clothing factory we broke into a few nights ago. I leave the room. Kyla watches me go.

Well, thank God for that. I could have said anything when I was delirious.

But I didn't mean to snap at her. I just didn't like what she said. If the best that can be said is that I'm the 'golden boy' of a creep like Zander, well, it doesn't say much. But it's true things have changed around here since I've been 'working' for him. Everyone has better clothes and gear and boxes of gadgets are starting to pile up in the rooms until Zander flogs them. And that's another worry, right there. I haven't heard anything further about this mate with the illegal chipping device. What if Zander decides I'm too valuable to let go? What then? I can't stay here forever. I feel like invisible arms are pulling me in all directions. I have to find out who I am. I'll never be able to live a normal life until I find out who that donor boy was and whether there's any connection with my own identity. But Jax is starting to feel like a real friend now too. And I've never had one of those before.

By the time I'm dressed, I'm regretting snapping at Kyla. I go back into the room, wondering what to say. But I stop dead in the doorway.

She's flicking round television channels. An Indian woman is serving behind the counter in a shop. It's some kind of soap by the looks of things. The image is so vivid because of the fancy 3D TV, it's like they're in the room. But suddenly I'm surrounded by feelings, smells, pictures, like I've been pitched headfirst into another world.

I see jars and jars of delicious sweets in rainbow colours. I'm pulling on a lady's skirt and whining. *I want those sweets so badly*.

And a woman is saying, 'Stop it, Cal! I told you, no sweets until Friday!'

I kick the counter in a temper, looking down at my feet. I'm wearing blue sandals. One of the leather straps is undone and my socks have Winnie the Pooh pictures on them.

'Matt? Matt? Are you all right?'

The room comes whooshing back into focus. Kyla is standing in front of me. Her hand tentatively touches my shoulder. 'What is it? What's wrong?'

I look up at her concerned face blearily. 'It's nothing,' I say, shakily. 'It's just . . . something I remembered.'

It's true. This is a *real* memory. Mine, from before the

time I was in the Facility. If I compare it with what I remember from my old life, it's like comparing a kid's drawing with the two-metre square, 3D television images in front of me. A smile spreads across my face and Kyla smiles back uncertainly.

'Matt,' she says finally. 'Tell me to mind my own business, but . . .'

'Mind your own business but . . .' I say quickly, but soften it with a smile. 'I'm OK, honest.'

She regards me for a minute and then shrugs. 'No worries. Least said, soonest mended, my mum used to say.' Something sad passes across her face. Then she looks up and brightens. 'Hey, you hungry, Matt?'

'Yeah, I am actually.' We live on takeaways here. I think about a greasy slice of hot cheesy pizza or some creamy chicken tikka massala and my mouth fills with spit. 'Shall I go get something?' There's a row of shops with a couple of takeaways back along the towpath.

'No need,' she says. 'I've been cooking.'

'Oh,' I say, forcing a rictus smile on my unwilling face. 'That's . . . great.'

She uncurls herself from the sofa in a way that looks like something you'd need to study for years and disappears from the room without saying anything else. I close my eyes and try to reach for more of the memory. But it's no good. It's like finding your way into a pitch dark room. It's gone.

I understand now why Amil's place has such a pull though. I've really been in that shop. Maybe his family will know who I am. But it would have been years ago.

Why would they remember me? It's all churning away inside my head as Kyla comes back into the room holding two steaming bowls.

'Budge,' she says and puts the bowls on the broken coffee table before flumping down next to me on the sofa.

'Er, thanks,' I say and she starts tucking into the food with a gusto you wouldn't expect from such a skinny girl who was recently at death's door. I peer into my bowl. It smells like something a cat coughed up on the pavement. I dip my spoon in and taste some, hesitantly. It's greasy, lumpy and a bit sour. Also, grey. I'm no expert but I'm guessing that's a bad colour for food.

'Like it?' says Kyla, watching me closely. 'It's potato and bacon soup. Well, sort of soup. Maybe more like a stew. Soup-stew. Stewp.' She laughs throatily and I feel a smile tickle my mouth. She turns serious again. 'Eat up! The bacon was a bit old, but I'm sure it's OK!' I decide that a boy who can fight his way out of a coma can guzzle down some bad soup. I spoon it down in about six massive gulps to get it over with. It has a taste and consistency not unlike that toxic canal water.

Kyla wipes her mouth with the back of her hand. Considering she's about the most elegant girl I've ever seen, she has some very trucker-like ways.

'Want some more?' she says hopefully.

'No! Er, I mean, no thanks. I'm all full up.' I pat my belly unconvincingly. 'It was . . . delicious.'

'Good, I'm glad you liked it, Matt. I wanted to do something nice for you. I wanted to . . .'

She looks down and presses a finger into a fag burn on the sofa like it's the most fascinating thing she's ever seen. 'Wanted to, you know . . .'

'What?' I say. My mouth has gone really dry but my hands are sweating. It's like all the moisture in my body is in the wrong places. She's sitting so close that I get a whiff of some sort of soap or perfume. It smells spicy and sweet, like cinnamon on apples. She looks up and my stomach dips, like I just jumped a ten storey building.

'Oh, you know, just wanted to say thanks. For saving my life.' She tries to sound flippant and does a silly wobble of her head. She has a tiny gap between her teeth and her tongue pokes through, pinkly. She couldn't look ugly, even if she tried really, really hard. Her skin is the colour of very milky coffee and I see her cheeks darken a bit. She smiles normally again and I notice her pupils, big and black in her chocolate brown eyes. Every bit of her face is just exactly right. I'd like to stare at it for three hours at least. My cheeks burn and I look away, clearing my throat.

'It's no problem,' I say in a strangled voice.

There's an awkward silence, then Kyla drums her thighs with her hands.

She gets up and gives a loud yawn. 'God, I'm going nuts in this place. I've got to get out of here for a while. Come for a walk with me?'

'Um, OK. Where to?' I wish I could stop umming and er-ing and speak normally.

'Just somewhere I like to go.'

Should I go with her? If she and Jax are . . . together or

something, maybe he wouldn't like us going off on walks all over the place. He's my friend. I don't want to tread on his toes . . .

But they don't *seem* like they're together. And it's only a walk, after all.

'Yeah, all right then,' I say, as though it's just one of many options I fancy just now.

'Right!' says Kyla, jumping nimbly to her feet. 'Let's clear this stuff away and get going.'

We leave a few minutes later, taking the back way through the estate. I haven't been this way before. There's some sort of a common with flooded roads to one side and a large patch of grass on the other. I can see a group of tower blocks in the distance and we head towards them. There's rubble everywhere, and piles of bricks. A digger with a massive wrecking ball is stark against the grey sky.

Even though the light's bleeding away by the second, it's good to get a quick glimpse of daytime. I've been living like some sort of bat recently. It's weird how quickly I've got used to my new life all the same. I've even adapted to the rotten air now. It's normal to see black stuff when I blow my nose and I'm used to having a bit of a cough. I sometimes long for things like a proper comfy bed and then I remember the only one I've ever really known was a hospital bed. That makes me feel a bit sick so I try to put it out of my mind and make myself comfortable on the floor. At least I'm free.

For now, anyway.

CHAPTER 22

better than starlight

Finally we come to the first of the tower blocks. Kyla flicks on the torch on her watch, which is identical to the one Jax has. I have two thoughts at once: that the watches are obviously from some job lot of stolen goods, and that I want one too. I make a mental note to ask Jax about this later.

The torch throws a splash of powerful white light onto the ground. Kyla looks up at the building ahead and I follow her gaze. Almost all the windows are broken. A pale sliver of moon is reflected in the few that still have glass, way up above us.

'Is *this* where we're going?' I say and she looks at me.

'Not good enough for you after Zander's Palace?' she says, her voice pulled hard and tight.

I swallow. She looks hurt. 'No, no, it's fine. Lead the way.'

Her face softens and then she flicks me a small smile.

We walk into a concrete stairwell that has a powerful smell of wee. This place makes my current home seem like the Ritz. Graffiti covers every bit of the walls and the grey metal lift door. Kyla presses a button on the wall and, incredibly, there's a juddering, clanking sound of movement from above.

The doors grind open. Somehow, the wee smell gets even stronger. Kyla steps inside the lift and sees my second's hesitation before I follow.

'It's all right,' she says. 'It works.'

The doors close.

'Sometimes, anyway,' she murmurs under her breath. She flashes me a wide grin then and I notice again the tiny gap between her front teeth. I can't understand why all girls don't want one exactly like it.

The lift complains and shakes slowly upwards then shudders to a stop. It feels like we've only gone about two floors but as we step out, I see a sign that says we're on Level 12.

'That's as far as it goes. We have to walk the next bit,' she says. 'Come on.'

We turn into the stairwell, which is littered with broken glass, and she stumbles. I catch her thin arm and our eyes meet in the gloom. I let go and we continue in silence.

I count ten more floors. I'm a little tired but Kyla is wheezing like mad.

'Look,' I say, stopping. 'Are you up to this?'

'I'm OK,' she says in a whisper. 'Nearly there now.'

I make myself slow down to her pace. After a couple

more floors we run out of stairs. We're obviously at the top. We turn into a row of flats with a long low balcony at the front. Most of the flats have metal doors across the front. I almost trip over a rusting child's bicycle and some old paint cans but Kyla seems to know this place well and moves quickly and easily. The very last flat has a normal front door with peeling, flaking paint. A brass number 1610 hangs lopsidedly. Kyla pulls a key out of her pocket and puts it in the lock. She has to shove the door hard with her shoulder to open it.

Inside, she sweeps the torch around, revealing a carpet covered in a swirly pattern. There's a strong damp smell and something scurries past my foot, making me scrunch my toes inside my trainers. The air feels cold and wind ruffles Kyla's hair.

She turns a corner off the small hallway.

I follow her and can't help sucking in my breath in surprise at what I see.

I'm in a large room, with windows that go almost floor to ceiling. Several of them have cracked glass or none at all but they curve round to give a panoramic view of the city below.

You can see for miles around. It's all glittering and twinkling like someone spread out a carpet of stars, just for us. Golden ropes of light mark the major roads and low flying helicopters swoop and dive with searchlights that criss-cross the city.

It's . . . beautiful. It feels like the whole world is down there, good and bad. A powerful feeling of being alive surges through me and I want to grab Kyla and hold her tight. How could I ever have thought that other world was real before? It was nothing like this really. I gaze at her instead and she smiles back.

'Like the view?' she asks, making a sweeping motion with her hand. 'It might be a long way up but this flat has the best view ever if you ask me.'

She walks over to an old sofa that faces out towards the windows and climbs on, wrapping her arms around her knees. She goes utterly still. I get a feeling that she's gone somewhere else entirely inside her head.

The wind howls through the window spaces in a ghostly chorus but it's weirdly soothing. It's cold up here but the air feels cleaner than any I've breathed since I came out of the Facility. I sit down on the sofa, the opposite end to Kyla. I'm careful not to sit too close, even though I want to. The material under me feels somehow greasy and crunchy at the same time.

'Is this where you used to live?' I say after a while.

Kyla stirs and looks at me. Her eyes are luminous in the semi-darkness. 'Yes,' she says and pauses for a moment before speaking again. 'Me and Mum. Flats were in a state even then, but no one wants to live in high rises now because everyone's scared of bombs. It's not going to be here in another week or two because they're pulling them down, one by one. I come back when I can. Just so I don't forget, you know?'

I nod. Do I know? I wish I did, which is close enough.

'Did you meet Jax here?' I say.

'No,' she says softly. 'Met him in care. We just sort of stuck together ever since.'

The question I've wanted to ask since I first met her slips out before I can stop myself. 'So you and him. Are you, er . . .'

Kyla lets out a throaty laugh. 'Shut *up*!' she says. 'That's disgusting! We're like *brother and sister*!'

'Oh,' I say, 'I thought . . .'

She curls her legs to the side. 'Nah,' she says, and looks at the window again. 'We just go back a long way, that's all.' I think about the way Jax looks at her when he thinks no one is watching. I'm not so sure he feels the same way. But I keep this to myself.

'Mum never really liked living here,' says Kyla dreamily. 'Wanted to live in the country. Somewhere with fields and cows!' She laughs like this is as crazy as wanting to live in the Sahara Desert. 'I'd rather have a bit of life. Although I'm sure there are better places than Sheffield.'

'How long did you live here?' I say carefully.

Kyla swallows and her fingers pluck at the bottom of her cardigan. 'Till I was ten,' she says. 'Then mum died of pig flu and I went into care. Hit this whole block really hard. Took Jax's parents too.'

'Pig flu?' It comes out as more of a question than I intended. 'What's that?'

This is definitely the wrong thing to say, judging by the scorching look on Kyla's face. 'How can you ask that?' she snaps. 'It killed half the bloody country. Where you been?'

I'm trying to think up some sort of excuse when something else comes out of my mouth instead.

'I was in an accident when I was little,' I say. 'I was in a coma for twelve years. The people who were monitoring me . . . they're bad, but I escaped. I'm a bit out of touch on some things. Sorry.'

Kyla is staring at me, lips parted and eyes wide.

'Close your mouth, princess, you'll catch flies,' I hear Des's voice clearly in my mind.

'So tell me about the pig flu,' I say hurriedly, to fill the silence.

'Wow,' says Kyla finally and clears her throat. 'Well. Wow! I don't know what to . . . Um . . . well, it happened five years ago. Started out as regular flu but then mutated in pigs or something. Mum was in the first load of people who got it.'

'Oh.' I rummage around for the right thing to say. 'Sorry,' I blurt, at last.

Kyla sighs and turns back to look out the window. It feels like ages before she speaks again. 'Yeah. It was rough. I still miss her every single day.' She pauses. 'What about you, Matt?' she turns to me, her eyes soft. 'Sounds like you've not exactly had an easy time either. Where are your parents?'

I look down. I have no idea how to reply to this question. Where are my parents? *Who* are they? Is there anyone out there who would claim me for their own?

I swallow deeply. 'I don't know,' I say at last. 'It's complicated. Do you mind if we don't talk about it?'

'No worries,' she says gently and turns back to look at the view.

'I've heard you can see stars in some places,' she says after a few moments. 'Not here though. Too much light pollution or something. But who needs stars when you've got all this, right?'

'Right,' I say quietly. We sit in silence, looking out at the jewel-studded darkness.

Suddenly there's a flash of light somewhere near the centre of the city, followed a couple of seconds later by a dull *crump* sound.

'Oh no!' Kyla jumps up and moves closer to the windows.

'What is it?

'Sounds like another plaster bomb,' she says. She turns to me. 'You don't know what those are either, right?'

I shrug and shake my head.

She explains. Things have moved on in the world of organised terror and suicide attacks aren't the way it's done now. Bombs are now sophisticated enough to fit on a small patch that looks a bit like a sticking plaster, hence the nickname. They're undetectable by any scanner. Every six months or so, one gets stuck onto the door of a commuter train or inside a café and activated by mobile. Then, as Kyla puts it, '*Kaboom.*'

'That's terrible,' I say and she nods, biting her lip. 'Who's behind them then?'

'Take your pick, there's about ten groups that usually say it was them. Often we hear it's a crowd called Torch, whoever they are.'

I have to chew my bottom lip to stop myself from speaking. I don't believe Torch have anything to do with the bombings. But I'm not getting into that now.

We watch clouds of smoke curl and twist into the night sky and in the distance sirens shriek and wail. Kyla moves back from the window and sits on the sofa and I sit down again too. I can't help noticing we're a bit closer than we were before.

I try to picture the aftermath of a bomb but all I see is the van with Tom and Nathan bursting into flames so I try to push it out of my mind. It's wrong, I know, but after a while, I start to feel a bit peaceful, sitting so high above the world with Kyla. Like all my problems are too small to make out, just like the cars and people so far below us.

I look around at the mouldering walls and damp carpet and, despite everything, I envy Kyla having this place. Also for having Jax as a 'brother' even if he doesn't exactly see it that way. I want to have that too. If there's anyone out there at all who knows me, I'm determined to find them if it's the last thing I do. It's not going to be easy to leave here though. I feel like I've made connections here. Like I'm not just someone's lab rat but someone with a good mate and a crush on a hot girl. Just a normal boy.

I sneak a look at Kyla. She curls her arm in and rests her head on it, away from me. A springy curl escapes and bounces up and I wonder what she would do if I gently pushed it back.

I'm going to do it.

I can't do it!

I'm going to, though.

I gather up all my courage, heart thumping and reach out my hand tentatively. She doesn't protest or move away. I touch her hair, very gently, and smooth it back from her face. She gives a little sigh. My heart bangs so hard in my chest I swear it must be booming loud enough for people on the ground to hear. I slide down the sofa a bit closer.

She said she and Jax weren't an item, right? But if I think about it too much I'll bottle it so I don't, I just lean a little bit closer again and close in . . . then hear a soft snore.

She's fast asleep.

CHAPTER 23

a substantial reward

I sit there for ages, just watching her. Feeling privileged that I can, in a funny way.

I don't remember falling asleep. But when my head jerks upright, a grey-pink stain is spreading up from the bottom of the sky into the darkness. Kyla is snuggled next to me now, her hair all bunched up under my chin in a way that tickles. My arm is around her and her slim brown hand, bitten nails painted with some purple sparkly stuff, is resting on my chest. I'm frightened to breathe, even though it looks like we've been like this for ages. She smells really good though. But her hair is tickling my nose and . . .

ATCHOO!

I sneeze explosively and Kyla's off the sofa like she's been shot from a cannon. She turns around, eyes wide, and then frowns, realising we've been snuggled up together all night. I'm a bit offended by how embarrassed she looks, as a matter of fact, like I've done something wrong. I get to my feet, trying to stretch out the kinks in my muscles.

'Morning.' I try to sound not bothered but I'm having a hard time meeting her eye.

She just grunts.

We don't speak on the way back to the house. I'm feeling a bit awkward about the whole falling asleep together thing. Maybe she is too. Or maybe it's not that. Maybe I'm just the very last person in the world she'd want to curl up with on a sofa and the thought turns sour in my belly like last night's evil soup. She probably prefers Jax, whatever she says. Who'd want someone who's never heard of pig flu and plaster bombs and probably a million other things?

All this swirls around inside me as we trudge back in the early morning light.

The house is quiet, apart from snores from the sleeping bodies draped everywhere. There are even more beer bottles than normal lying around and the carpet crunches. Looks like they've had a party. The air reeks of feet and a sweetish smoke.

I go into the kitchen and pour some suspect-looking juice into a cup before downing it in one go. There's a left-over naan bread from a takeaway on the side and I eat it in a few bites.

Kyla comes into the kitchen, her skin with a freshly-scrubbed glow that makes her look really young. She avoids my eye and drinks some water straight from the tap. Exhaustion trickles inside my bones. All I want is to curl up under a blanket and sleep but Zander seems to appear from nowhere. His eyes are bloodshot and starey. I know he's taken something by the way he sways against the doorframe.

'Well, lookie here,' he says thickly. 'If it isn't the invisible man.'

'Uh . . . morning, Zander.' I try to leave the room but he's barring the way. He's way taller than me but I stand firm and meet his glassy eyes, trying not to breathe in the chemical tang on his breath.

'Who'd have thought it, eh?' he says.

'What?' I say, confused.

Zander gets out his phone and, still smiling, touches the screen and then points it at the kitchen wall. A tanned woman with stiff blond hair is sitting on a desk in 3D. *Terrorism Alert* runs along the bottom of the screen before she speaks.

'Police are asking the general public to look out for a teenage boy, believed to be behind the latest terrorist atrocity, a so-called "plaster bomb" that went off in an inner city branch of Starbucks last night.'

My guts loop-the-loop as a picture appears on the screen. It's my face. The mug shot was obviously taken from the Facility because I have a weird, spaced-out look. Exactly the kind of look you might expect from a mad terrorist.

'Police say the boy has been radicalised by a terrorist organisation known as Torch, who have been involved in violent anti-government protests for several years. He is described as unstable and potentially dangerous. There' s a substantial reward for any member of the public whose information leads to the boy's arrest. Here's that number again . . .'

I can't breathe. Pictures hurtle into my mind. I'm lying in a hospital bed, drugged and powerless again, wires everywhere. Unable to move, unable to think for myself. Or in a cell, somewhere like Riley Hall. Left to rot. I'm making little gasping sounds and the walls start to pulse around me again like sheets of cardboard being rippled. I'm not letting them catch me. Not when I've had exactly ten days of freedom and had a glimpse of a proper life. And I've still got to get to Brinkley Cross and find Amil. Then trace my family. It can't end now, can it? Not like this. The image snaps off and Zander smiles, showing his pointy teeth. 'Well, well, well . . .' he says.

'You know I had nothing to do with that!' I say in a kind of rough squeak.

Kyla speaks at the same time. 'I was with Matt last night. He didn't even know what plaster bombs were until I told him!'

'Do you think I'm stupid?' Zander's voice is soft and he's not smiling any more. 'I couldn't care less about no bomb. I don't even care why they really want you. You've been useful to me. But I'm thinking a *substantial reward* is better than a few knock-off DVDs and some crates of booze. You see my dilemma?'

There's no time to waste.

I slam my shoulder into Zander as hard as I can. Because he's drugged up, it takes him by surprise and he falls back against the work surface. I run for the front door.

Kyla screams, 'Run, Matt!'

I'm out into the estate, darting around the nearest corner, looking around wildly. Zander knows the shortcuts like the back of his hand. Crashing into brick and grazing my hands, I shuttle around corners, trying to put distance between me and the house. Gasping for breath, I start to recognise the buildings that mark the edge of the estate.

I get my breath and run out into the open ground. Then something slams into me so hard that all the air leaves the world and darkness swirls around me. I can see Zander's crazed face above me, eyes mad with fury as he raises his booted foot. Pain knifes into my side. Everything is red, angry, hurting. I spit blood onto the scraggy grass and some distant part of me thinks, 'He's going to kill me now.' Images of Pigface get all mixed up in what's happening and I'm not even certain who it is hitting me . . .

There's a thud and Zander crumples like a dead weight on top of me, his greasy blond hair fanned next to my face. His eyes are closed.

Retching and gasping for breath, I manage to shove him away. Kyla stands above us, a broken bottle in one hand and the other over her mouth. It takes a second for my brain to put the pieces together. Kyla hit him. He was going to kill me and Kyla stopped him. She saved me.

She starts to cry and drops the bottle, then just runs.

'Kyla,' I say thickly but she's gone. For a horrible minute I think maybe she believes that story. But no, she defended me, didn't she? She knows I have nothing to do with that bomb.

I groan. I'm hurting so badly, I can't get up and it takes

me ages to struggle to my feet. I don't think Zander's dead, although he looks bad. I lean over him and put my fingers to the side of his neck like I know what I'm doing. There's definitely something fluttering in there. I don't know whether I'm relieved or not. I spit more blood onto the ground and gently touch my lip, which feels spongy and wet.

I hear approaching footsteps and have no time to move before Kyla is there again. She has Jax with her. She's still crying hard. Jax's eyes go round when he sees Zander and he leans over him, then looks at me.

'What the . . . ? What did you do to Zander, man?'

'I did it!' shrieks Kyla and I look around nervously. 'He was gonna kill him, Jax!'

Jax puts his hands in his hair and paces up and down, saying, 'Oh, man, this is bad,' over and over again.

'We need to get out of here.' It hurts to talk. My tongue feels too big and my teeth don't fit. They both nod vigorously, as though I'm suddenly in charge.

Think, Cal, think!

'Go get whatever you need; money, clothes,' I say. 'We'll meet you by the flats. Quickly, Jax! Tell anyone you see that we're on an urgent job. GO!'

Jax runs off.

Kyla is holding her elbows and staring down at Zander, who is still out cold. She looks up at me slowly.

'Is he dead?'

'No,' I say, like I'm certain. 'Kyla, come on. We have to get away from here.'

We hurry in silence to the meeting place. I have to breathe in small sips because of the screaming pain in my ribs.

Jax is there within five minutes. His eyes are still wide and a muscle is twitching in his cheek. 'Oh, man, this is so messed up,' he says. He puts his hands on his head and turns round in a circle. 'I think I'm going to go see if I can sort this.'

Kyla slaps him hard on the chest. 'What's wrong with you?' she hisses. 'He's going to kill me when he comes round! And you don't even know what happened! Matt's *wanted*, man! They're trying to blame him for a bomb!'

Jax's eyes go wide. 'What you talking about?' he says. 'Why?'

I stare at him helplessly. I don't even know where to begin. 'It's . . . complicated.'

'Complicated? You bet it's complicated!' shouts Jax. 'What are we going to do? Where are we gonna go, Matt?'

'Matt's not my real name.'

I hear Kyla's sharp intake of breath.

'I'm called Cal,' I continue. 'I escaped from somewhere bad and the authorities want me back. I'm . . . valuable to them. They'll do anything, say anything, to get me.'

There's a heavy silence. I blink hard, trying to stop tears from leaking out.

Just as I've found people I care about, I'm going to have to leave them.

I meet eyes with Kyla. A Revealer Chip isn't always necessary to see inside someone. She already knows what I'm thinking.

'He's got to leave us, Jax,' she says softly. 'We can't stay with him. It's not safe.'

She doesn't take her eyes off mine. We stare at each other for ages. I hear Jax cough and when I look at him, suspicion flashes across his face.

'Where was you, anyway?' he says.

'What?' says Kyla sharply, her face scornful.

'What are you *talking* about. This is serious, man!' I say.

'Last night. Where was you?' says Jax, moving a bit closer to her.

She snorts, disgustedly, and steps away, crossing her arms. 'I wanted to show him the flat. You got a problem with that? You're not the boss of me, Jax! And we got more important things to think about now!'

Jax starts to say something else and I interrupt him.

'It's not like that,' I say. 'We just fell asleep, that's all.'

Jax tips his chin and narrows his eyes.

I make a frustrated huffing sound. It makes my busted lip hurt more.

'Where will you go, M— Cal?' says Kyla.

I stare at my shoes. 'I've got to find a place called Brinkley Cross,' I say after a moment. 'It's not that far. But I've got to try to change my appearance first. There are pictures of me everywhere. Will you help?'

Kyla says she knows what to do and disappears off to a chemist. She comes back with a small paper bag a few minutes later.

We find some public toilets whose floor is crunchy with

broken glass and litter. The smell is horrible in there and the tap water's brown but it'll do. Kyla hacks at my hair with nail scissors. Then I wet it under the freezing, smelly water and she applies the dye. The colour is called *Cocoa Kisses* on the box. Stupid, that I notice that. It's dark brown, anyway, as far as I can tell. Changing how I look, that's what counts.

Someone tries to come down when we're halfway through. Jax, who's guarding the stairs, says, 'Sorry, suspect device found here. Police on their way.' I hear panicky footsteps skittering back up the steps.

We don't really speak during the whole process, apart from the odd 'Move that way' or 'Head back' from Kyla. Jax keeps staring at me like he's seeing me for the first time. Maybe that's how it feels. He keeps looking at Kyla too. I want to know what he's thinking, and at the same time I don't.

I'm miserable, cold and wet by the time she's done. After rubbing my head a bit on the filthy hand towel, I look in the mirror. I'm not sure I look different enough. It's clearly me behind the freaked-out eyes and dark, spiky hair, even with the fat lip and purple bruise on my cheek. Some of the dye has trickled down my neck leaving brown stains. I rub at them for ages but the towel just makes them worse.

I think quickly about how to get out of Sheffield. I'll go to the motorway services on the edge of the city that I saw with Tom, then hitch a ride. I noticed a load of lorries there last time. One of them must be heading in the direction of Brinkley Cross.

Outside the toilets, Jax tells me how to get there. It's not far. I can keep to the backstreets. I've started to learn a bit about this city on my night jaunts with Zander.

'Thanks. For everything,' I say. 'And I'm really sorry. I didn't mean to mess things up for you both.'

We stand there, the three of us, shuffling our feet and no one looking at anyone else. A light rain starts to patter on our shoulders. My head feels cold and exposed with my new short hair.

I open my mouth to say something else and Jax pulls me into a bear hug so tight I can't breathe. My bruised ribs scream with angry pain but that's not the only reason my eyes prickle and burn. I have to squeeze them tightly closed. He releases me and looks at his feet. A weird, out-of-place happiness that he forgives me for getting too close to Kyla warms me inside for a moment.

'It's not too late for us to come,' he says. 'We could still —'

'No,' I say, shaking my head, voice wobbling. 'It's not safe for you. The people who want me are really bad. You two need to carry on looking out for each other. Just like before.'

They exchange glances. Kyla's eyes shine and she wipes a hand across her nose. Then she sniffs loudly and straightens her back. 'Come on, Jax,' she says. 'There's no point hanging about. We've got to find somewhere else to stay.'

She avoids my eye. If I thought – hoped – there would be any hugs from her, I was wrong. It's maybe for the best. I'm not sure I can go through with this if I touch her and smell her cinnamon smell again.

'Let's go,' she says, and takes him by the hand. 'Bye, Matt, I mean, Cal. Take it easy.' If it wasn't for the way she swallows and keeps blinking, you'd think she wasn't feeling anything at all right now.

I mumble, 'Yeah, you too,' and turn away first. It feels like something inside has been ripped out, leaving a raw, open wound. I walk fast, head down and don't look back. Without making a conscious decision to do it, I start to run, ignoring the thumping pain in my ribs and the wetness on my face that isn't rain.

I feel like a great howl inside me is trying to break free so I run faster, harder, and don't stop.

They were the only real friends I've ever had. All I brought them was trouble.

And now I'm alone again.

Chapter 24

bruises

It doesn't take that long to reach the motorway services. Keeping my head down, I go inside and buy juice, a sandwich and some crisps, trying not to look as guilty and conspicuous as I feel.

I walk towards the lorry car park.

Footsteps pound behind me then and someone calls out. I drop the bag of food and spin round, looking for somewhere to run. They can't have traced me already, can they? I look around wildly for something I can use as a weapon but there's no time because someone is already right there, next to me.

'Hey, you!' It's a bloke in his twenties with a shaved head and loads of earrings around his lobes. A row of jewels sparkle under his bottom lip and a silver bolt is through his eyebrow with a little chain on the end. He's wearing some sort of overall and gasping for breath. 'You forgot your change!' he says, leaning forward with his hands on his knees. I finally recognise the man who served me in the shop.

I burst out laughing. I don't know if it's a release of tension after everything that's happened or if I'm just losing it, but I laugh so hard I have to lean against the wall and get my breath back.

The bloke just watches me, smiling uncertainly. I eventually get myself together and take the money from his hand. 'Sorry,' I say. 'And thanks for this.'

'Been one of those days, has it, mate?' he says. His eyes flick from my cheek to my lip.

'Yeah,' I say, 'you could say that.'

After two hours of hanging around in the car park I start realising this was a stupid plan all along. I'd pictured lorry drivers standing around talking and me picking up useful information about where they're going. But it's nothing like that. People come and go but no one speaks to anyone else. They just pull in, get out, and come back with burgers, sandwiches and boxes of fried chicken. Then they get back into their lorries to eat them before driving off with a dismissing hiss of hydraulic brakes.

After a while, though, I finally get some much-needed luck. A massive blue and white lorry with *John Hartman and Sons, Office Supplies* on the side pulls into the car park. It also says *Brinkley Cross, Lancashire* on the back. Result! I just have to hope it's heading that way. I don't even know which side of the road, I am – north or south.

I wait, crouching at the back of the lorry until I hear the doors slam and the driver walk away. He's on his mobile phone. Sounds like he's telling his wife what time he'll be back. They're bickering because it's later than he promised, but he's on his way back.

Result.

It's the first decent thing that's happened to me in ages. I creep to the back of the lorry and reach into my pocket for the lock picks that Zander gave me. The first few don't fit and I'm swearing a bit under my breath as I try to find one that does.

That's when I hear voices and a horrible wet, panting sound.

I peek out to see the bloke with the piercings, flanked on each side by CATS officers wearing black crash helmets with the visors up. The piercings guy is pointing to where we had our conversation. My heart thuds and acidy fear jolts every part of me. Did he report me?

They start to walk over and that's when I notice the huge, slavering Alsatian dog on a lead in the CATS officer's hand. He can barely control it and the dog pulls and strains with its powerful body, tongue lolling and vicious teeth bared. They start checking underneath lorries, the dog making itself flat to sniff underneath. I start praying, silently, my fingers slippery with sweat as I fumble with one and then another of the lock picks. The whole bunch then slides out of my hand and hits the concrete, making the loudest sound in the history of the world, ever. I snatch them up and the very last one fits with a wonderful, fantastic *click.*

I fling open the doors, panting, and get inside, softly closing the door behind me. The voices are getting closer and now they must be checking the lorries in the parking row next to this one. I climb behind a load of boxes, crouching down and shaking hard. I watch the doors, expecting them to be flung open any second with an explosion of snarling teeth.

But, thank God, I hear the driver's voice again then. He's still arguing on his phone. He doesn't check the back. I hear the cabin door slam. Everything rumbles around me and the powerful machine comes to life.

I huddle between the boxes, longing to sleep but knowing I have to stay alert. Every time I feel my head loll or my eyes droop, I make myself press against my busted lip or my throbbing cheek. The agony brings me back to consciousness like an electric cattle prod.

Have to think. Have to make a plan. I put my head between my hands and try to conjure up the images of Brinkley Cross that are stored somewhere in my brain. Have to get to Amil's place. He'll be what, mid-twenties now? That thought is so freaky it makes me draw in my breath. Of course he won't know me. His mum and dad won't know me. I'm a total stranger to them. But I know I've been inside their shop. It's not much, but it's a tiny link in the chain that connects to my real identity. If I can make them listen to my crazy story, surely they'll help me? Maybe they'll even remember a small boy called Cal. My heart races again and I can't stop a smile from coming to my sore face at the thought of finding a real family of my own. But if I do have one, why didn't anyone ever get me out of that place? This makes the smile fade and a chill settle inside. I don't know the answers to any of these questions yet. But maybe I'm getting closer to finding them.

The engine sounds change after a while and the lorry slows down. It seems to twist and turn for ages. The pain in my ribs is getting worse, like someone is turning up the volume. I peel back the bandage on my hand and wince at the swollen skin around the cut. It's red and weirdly firm to the touch. That can't be right. I put back the bandage. A little infection is the least of my worries right now.

Finally the lorry stops with a sort of rumbling sigh. I creep further back behind the boxes and a horrible thought occurs to me. What if I have to stay here all night, locked in? But no, there's a sound of metal on metal and the doors open.

I pull back further behind the boxes.

A metal ramp is being lowered and then the lorry shakes as someone climbs inside. I swear they can hear my heart-beat, which seems to be booming around the metal walls on loudspeaker.

There's some huffing and puffing and then the floor bounces gently as the driver walks down the ramp.

I can't wait any longer. I just have to do it.

As his footsteps recede and I hear him talking to some-one in the distance, I get up and run down the ramp. I'm in a loading bay at the back of a factory and the gates are open. I put my head down, hands in my pockets and walk towards the gates, trying not to attract attention to myself.

'Hey! Where the hell did you come from?'

The shout feels like an explosion behind me and I run, hard, out of the gates and into an industrial estate where large metal warehouses loom all around. I keep running, following the side of the road and then come to a stop, gasping for breath at the edge of the estate. I risk a quick glance behind. No one seems to be following me. I'm facing a roundabout that shows Brinkley Cross railway station as being straight ahead. Dark clouds are clumping together as I walk along the side of the country road. There's a wall made from rough grey stone at each side and dark green and purplish hills rear up all around. Everything is the colour of bruises.

I'm about to get moving when something makes me stop, dead still. I sniff the air. I sniff again and close my eyes as a powerful feeling of recognition washes over me, sweet and warm like honey. There's a rich hoppiness in the air that's so familiar, it feels like it's part of my DNA. It's the brewery! The donor boy could see the brewery from his house on the hill. But this is nothing to do with slivers of brain tissue and second-hand memories. This is *my* memory. Mine!

That's when I know for certain that Brinkley Cross is not just his, but my town too. I'm home.

CHAPTER 25

shutters

I'm grinning like a madman but my eyes are filling up and a funny sob comes out of me. I rub my hand across my battered, sore face and squeeze my eyes closed. I get a stupid urge to tell Jax and Kyla and then I remember I can't; they've gone, and sadness twists inside me. I take a deep breath. My legs are wobbly and my face is burning like I've been too long in the sun. I feel a bit weird. But I guess it's no wonder after the last day or so. I take a deep breath and clench, then unclench my fists. I'm ready.

Right, first stop: Amil's shop. I have to hope they won't think I'm a nutter and slam the door in my face. I'll have to watch my step too. I look around. No CCTV here but there are bound to be cameras in the town. It's broad daylight so I can't exactly use my training from working with Zander's lot or I'll draw even more attention to myself. Just have to wing it. I can't give up now. I have no options anyway. A memory of Cavendish's voice comes to me. What did he say? 'Mixing the two realities – the world of your coma and the real world – is just not advisable. Anything could go wrong'. Now I know why he said that. He didn't want me anywhere near my home town. Asking questions and finding out where I came from. Maybe finding my family.

I pull up my hood, shove my hands in my pockets and start walking.

I soon come to the edge of the town. I can see another sign for the railway station ahead. My heart starts to thump. I rub my damp palms on my trousers, wincing as I remember the puffy wound on my hand. My eyes hurt and I feel out of breath. Was Cavendish telling the truth? Was coming here a mistake?

I don't care anyway. I need to find out who I am. No matter what it costs.

I walk past the station, which has hanging baskets outside that sway gently in a light breeze that's blowing. Something tugs at the back of my mind, a memory of looking up at baskets like these from much lower down. Excitement throbs in my chest.

I pass a flower shop and then a betting shop. I know I'm not far from Amil's shop now. I can feel it. It's up ahead where the road curves. I go faster, praying silently that Amil's family will believe my story. There are a few people milling around, going about their ordinary days. I feel a stab of envy and wonder what it would be like to be normal, like them. That's all I want. A home. A family. A normal life.

I avoid catching anyone's eye anyway, not wanting to draw attention to myself, and hurry on, shaking now with anticipation. Almost there . . .

And then my feet slow to a stop.

The world shrinks to a small, choking thing.

The shop as I know it has gone.

A metal concertina shutter covers the windows and doors. Faded graffiti is daubed over the brickwork and most of the windows are smashed. I go close to the metal shutter and rest my burning hands and face against it. Inside I can see empty shelves covered in cobwebs and dirt. Broken glass litters the ground.

'Excuse me, pet.' The voice behind me is quivery and low. I start and look round to see an old lady peering at me. She has dyed black hair piled in a bun on her head with lots of pins in it. 'You don't want to spend too long there. You never know who might be watching you.' She looks around nervously and her tongue creeps over her pink lipstick.

'What . . .' I have to make a huge effort to find my voice. 'What happened to the shop?'

She looks around again and pats her hair. 'They left. Think they got deported or something, which was a crying shame because that lad of theirs was born and bred here. CATS kept pulling him in and questioning him like he was some sort of terrorist.' She puffs out her chest. 'But I told them, I said, they're good people, I said. There's no call to go interrogating innocent people like them.' She pauses and gives a ripe smoker's cough. 'But they wouldn't listen to me,' she adds sadly.

I stare desperately at the front of the shop. The familiar sign saying *Sweet Stop* ripples and blurs. I squeeze my eyes closed and then open them again.

'Did they leave any kind of an address?' I ask hopelessly. 'Do you know how I can contact them?'

The old lady shakes her head. 'No, pet. One day they were here, then they were gone. Look, you don't want to go hanging around on the streets. Like I said, you never know who's watching you. Best get off to where you come from.' She pats my arm and then bustles away, clutching a huge black handbag to her side.

Where I come from . . .

I want to punch something. Or someone. Hard. This was my only hope of finding out where that was. I went through so much to get here and for what? Nothing?

I walk away, hands in my pockets and my head down. *This isn't fair. Not fair!* Everything is wobbling and closing in around me and I can hear my breath coming in and out, harsh and scratchy. I'm not frightened now. I'm so angry I could do anything. To have come all this way and risked so much . . . An empty lager can lies at the side of the road and I kick it savagely. A bloke washing a shop front across the way stares at me with a quick frown. I scowl back at him and walk on, not knowing where I'm going, too upset and angry to care what anyone thinks.

My furious footsteps slap against the pavement. I keep walking, clenching and unclenching my fists and not even caring about the pain in my injured one. After a few minutes I come to the end of the road. It's a cul-de-sac with a church and large graveyard set back from the road. I walk blindly through the ornate wooden gate. I need to be alone for a minute with no one watching. Or do they even monitor people praying these days? I wouldn't put anything past these people. I kick at the gravel furiously, bristling with frustration and disappointment.

I find a bench and sit down on the end, resting my head in my hands. I have no idea what to do next. No plan. No ideas. The thought that Amil's family might help me was my only hope.

Self-pity and tiredness roll over me. Hopeless tears prickle my eyes. I have nowhere to go now. No one who might be able to help me find out who I am. I groan and look up, eyes stinging, and take a couple of deep breaths to try to calm myself. It smells of dampness and rich green moss, but the brewery smell is always there in the background. So familiar, but it doesn't bring me any answers.

Home, but not home.

A man in overalls with a wheelbarrow appears at the far end of the graveyard. I see him glance at me. I pretend to be looking at the gravestones, like I have a reason to be here. Don't want to make him suspicious.

Names and dates swim in front of my eyes. Some of the graves have fresh flowers on them. Others have plastic ones. One has an old teddy, which sits forlornly against the pale grey stone, years of weather and dirt etched into its synthetic fur.

I glance up and see the man with the wheelbarrow looking over again. I move to another grave, like I'm really interested. I'll wait until he turns away and then get out of here.

I stare down at the white stone, which has flecks of black all over it, but I'm not really seeing it. I'm thinking about the donor boy now and wondering if his gravestone is here too. My hand goes to my scar. And then it feels as though electricity screams through my body, from the soles of my feet to the top of my head.

I look properly at the words swimming in front of me.

I blink, just in case my eyes are playing tricks, and look again.

No. This is real. I'm not imagining what I'm seeing . . .

The gravestone in front of me has a name and a date, with an inscription that reads, *Beloved son, sleep in peace*.

But it isn't some stranger's name on the grave.

It's mine.

Chapter 26

a debt

C*allum Michael Conway* is etched into the stone. The dates are 4th January 2010 – 17th June 2012.

I'm panting and sweat trickles between my shoulder blades. I reach out and trace the letters with a finger. Something drips off my chin and I realise I'm crying without even realising it.

I'm looking at my own grave.

'Cal Conway,' I whisper.

Now I know why no one came to look for me at the Facility. They believed I was dead. But why? How did this happen? Questions batter me from all sides.

I look down. There are flowers growing in two small tubs in front of the gravestone. I don't know anything about plants but these don't look neglected to me. It looks like someone comes here and looks after this grave.

Beloved son.

My parents? Do my parents come here? I look around wildly. Something light is filling me up inside and I'm grinning so hard suddenly it's like my face will split open with happiness even though I'm crying at the same time.

I'll find them here. If it takes a year, I'll wait until someone comes. I'll watch and wait and then I'll find the people who care about me.

The old man with the wheelbarrow is coming my way. OK, so I need to make a move. The last thing I want is to draw attention to myself now, right when I might be getting close to finding the truth.

I walk confidently towards him, as though I have nothing to hide. I nod, and he nods back. I can feel his eyes on my back as I walk out of the graveyard and back into the street outside. I feel three times lighter than I did when I went in. Changed inside. Everything is different now. I've got a reason to hope again.

Right, so I'll stay away for a little while, just so I can avoid that bloke working there. Then I'll come back and find a good hiding place. And then I'll wait.

I don't care how long it takes. I'll just wait until someone comes to that grave.

I go back into the high street. There are more people around now, shopping, pushing buggies and talking to squabbling children. I want to smile at them and talk. Tell them I have a family too. But I force myself to remember the nature of the world I'm in.

I glance up to see if I can make out the CCTV cameras

on the buildings and see them straight away. There are far less here than in the city; only one or two. It's easy to circumvent their probing gaze without looking shifty.

I've still got a little money so I buy a pastie and a can of drink from a bakery then walk along, eating it. My hand throbs with a steady rhythm and I wish I had the painkillers Helen Bonaparte gave me, but they're back at Zander's place. That brings uncomfortable thoughts and worries about Jax and Kyla, so instead I try to think about what to do next.

I walk past a school and a ticklish feeling of familiarity makes me gasp. I know this school. It's the donor boy's school. It's breaktime. Kids play football, or hunch in groups laughing over phones. Just being normal teenagers. They don't know how lucky they are.

Pictures from my old life – or what I thought was my life – flit across my mind. I know my name but I still don't know the donor boy's. What a life. Being bullied by Des and Pigface and then dying young. A feeling of sadness and injustice burns in my chest.

Before I go back and hide in the graveyard, there's something I need to do. I ball up the pastie bag and can and throw them into a bin. I need to find out what happened to him. I owe him that.

CHAPTER 27

a different boy

My feet seem to know where to go. I go past some more shops and through a few alleys. I avoid catching anyone's eye, keeping my hood up and taking notice of the occasional CCTV camera. Before long, I come out at the bottom of a huge hill with countryside lying all around. I look up.

Sitting there on the top of the hill, just like Des's zit, is the house.

It's quiet but I'm breathing heavily, like I've been running. I'm sweating all over, but shivery too. My hand hurts really badly now. I pull down the bandage and see the skin all round the wound is puffy and there's a strange dark line coming from the wound into my wrist. Still, there's nothing I can do about it.

I look around, feeling exposed now there are no buildings,

but there are no cameras here either. Jax trained me well and I know how to spot even the hidden ones.

No one knows me in that house. But I need to do this for him, the boy who gave me his memories.

I walk up the hill.

When I get close, I slow down involuntarily, nerves tugging at my guts. I stare at the house as fear and excitement and something else mingle together.

The place looks even worse than the image in my head. A couple of the windows are broken and most of the paint has peeled off the window frames and front door. A filthy grey net curtain has escaped from a hole in one of the upstairs windows and is fluttering in the wind like a ripped old flag. I move closer until I'm standing right in front of the house.

Words can't describe how this feels.

It's home.

It's not home.

I know every inch of it.

I've never been here.

Suddenly I get a big lump in my throat and have to sit down on a greasy old deckchair out front. I want to just blub everywhere as sadness overwhelms me for the boy who lived in this miserable house. I put my head in my hands and try to breathe slowly. I feel sorry for myself and I feel sorry for him. Living here with a mum who didn't really care. With a fat bully like Des and that evil little —

'Who the hell are you?'

My head jerks up.

It can't be.

'Des?'

He's so bloated it looks like someone blew him up with a bicycle pump. His nose is covered in broken red veins and his eyes have almost disappeared into the doughy folds of his cheeks. He's unshaven and wearing a stained yellow jumper with nothing underneath so it clings to his man boobs. Grey hair pokes out of the V under his double chin. He sways slightly. He's drunk. His hand creeps into his trouser pocket.

'Who the hell are you?' he repeats, stumbling slightly.

'Don't you know me, Des?' A strange feeling of energy is pulsing through me. I feel strong and I find myself flexing my one good fist.

He screws up his face, bottom lip hanging open and glistening with spit.

I walk over to him. Maybe he glimpses what I'm feeling because he takes a step back, his eyes revealing something I've never seen in them before.

Fear.

To him I'm just some young hoodie. I could be anyone. He's made enough enemies in his life. I'm young and strong and he's old and fat and powerless.

I'm filled with emotions that feel like helium. It's all I can do not to laugh hysterically.

I move closer and he takes another step and then trips over an old car tyre. He cries out and lands with a heavy grunt on his fat backside. He tries to get up but he's stuck, flailing around helplessly, like a turtle the wrong way up.

He waves his feet, which are puffy and swollen in old Nike sandals, his toenails yellow like old ivory.

'Where is everyone?' I say. 'Your family?'

'All gone away,' he says breathlessly. 'Left me.' He swears.

'What happened to your stepson, Des?'

He flaps around and manages to struggle to his feet. He waves his fist but is so drunk he can hardly stand and I feel no threat at all.

Not any more.

'Don't you mention that boy to me!' he says in a strangled voice. 'Ryan nearly died after what he did! Deserved everything he got!'

'What? What do you mean? What did he do?'

'Hit my boy so hard he almost killed him, that's what!' spits Des. 'Got what he deserved, the ungrateful little toerag! Served him right that he got banged up!'

I gasp as a memory comes into my head with perfect detail. Ryan attacking me. Knowing he was going to kill me. Reaching for the football trophy at the side of the bed . . . I know what happened next. Except it wasn't me. It was a different boy, who never really had a chance, living here.

'What was his name?' I hiss.

I see Des's stubbly chin glisten with nervous sweat. 'Why do you want to know?'

I shove him hard on the chest and he cries out. 'Tell me his name,' I say slowly, my voice low.

'A-Alex,' he says shakily. 'His name was Alex.'

'And how did he die?'

Des's hand reaches into his tracksuit pocket and I stiffen, but all he does his bring out a manky old tissue, which he uses to wipe his chin with a trembling hand.

'Don't know. Some accident in Riley Hall. Good riddance, it was! I did nothing but take that boy in and treat him like my own, and that's how he repaid me!'

'I'll tell you what you did,' I hiss into his face, wincing at the smell on his breath. 'You bullied him and humiliated him and frightened him. And so did Ryan! He hit him in self-defence!'

His expression hardens. 'Who the hell are you, anyway? What do you know about it? He was worthless, that little sod! Worthless!'

I've heard people say they see red when they lose it. I lose it now but I don't see red.

This is for you, Alex, I think.

All I can see is Des's fat, frightened face moving from side to side.

I hit him, once, twice, three times. Blood blossoms on his lip and nose and I feel so powerful I could keep going for ever. I could kill him, this fat, pathetic man. I'm the one with muscles and speed and youth on my side. I'm the stronger one now.

And then I think, *Who's the bully now?*

I step back, trying to get my breath, hands on my knees. He's sobbing quietly. I hold out my hand. 'Get up,' I say tightly. I'm disgusted with him, but more than that, I'm disgusted with myself.

He takes my hand with his meaty, sweaty one and a nasty smile spreads across his face as he hauls himself to his feet. Before he lets go, he does an odd thing, and puts his hand on my back as though patting me.

We stand close, eyeballing each other. I'm not frightened of him now. I pity him. I turn away and walk back down the hill. When I get to the bottom, I look back up and he's gone.

I'm trembling all over and my head's throbbing along with my hand, but I don't regret going there. I still don't know how Alex became the brain tissue donor but I know it had something to do with Riley Hall.

I walk back into the town. I only have one thought now. I'm going back to the graveyard and I'm going to wait there until someone visits that grave.

Until my family comes.

It takes less than ten minutes to get back there. This time I come in carefully, scanning for the gravedigger bloke or whoever he was. There are loads of tall hedges and bushes and I stay close to them, using all my training to stay in the shadows.

I find somewhere to hunker down, behind a big old grave from seventeen-something that's covered in bright green ivy. I settle down and wait.

And wait.

It gets colder by the minute and a light rain starts to fall. I swear, feeling pitifully sorry for myself. No one's coming here. I'm stupid to think I'll find anyone this way . . .

And then my heart flips over. There's someone there. A woman in a bright green coat is going over to the grave. My grave. She's bending down. Her hair is a faded red and her curls bob as she works away at pulling out weeds around the headstone.

Oh my God. It can't be. Can it?

Is that my mother?

Am I really looking at my own mum?

I don't want to freak her out by running to her and anyway, my legs are shaking so violently that I can hardly stand up. I can hear someone crying and realise it's me. Tears slide down my face. I'm smiling and crying at the same time.

I must have made a noise because she starts and then turns to look at me. She gets up hastily and I realise I have my hood pulled up high. Maybe she thinks I'm a mugger. She starts to gather her things to leave and I cry out.

'No! Don't go!' I pull the hood back from my face and watch her look of fear turn to confusion.

'It's me!' I say, my voice cracking and wobbling all over the place.

She scrunches her brow, studying me for what seems ages. She gives her head a little shake and smiles, then frowns again. Her lips part and make the shape for 'What?' but it's soundless. Then her eyes go wide and her hands fly to her face. She gives a little cry.

We both start to move at once but a droning, violent sound suddenly fills the air around me and suddenly I'm surrounded by black metal things, buzz drones, crowding like angry bees. All I can see is my own terrified face reflected back in their bug-like eyes. I wave my arms and something small and black falls to the ground. I think, *A tracker. Des put a tracker on my back. They've got me.*

She starts to come towards me and I manage to shout 'Run! They'll take you too! RUUUN!' It's the last thing I know before electric agony blasts everywhere around and there's only white pain, blotting out the world.

Part III

CHAPTER 28

circles

I come to on the floor of a van. My cheek is pressed against the cold metal and I'm bound by metal ropes around my wrists and feet so I can't move. A sob wrenches my throat.

I was so close.

So very close to being with my family.

The tears come properly then, pouring down my cheeks, despite the blinking light of a camera on the door, an evil eye that watches my every move. I bawl until I'm empty inside and I can taste dried salt. I lie there, getting bumped and battered by every movement of the van. My vision is funny and I'm hot then cold then hot again. I see Des's face leering at me with a cigarette between his teeth and cry out because it feels like he really is there. Then I see Pigface, but his face changes into Jax's then Kyla's and both are crying.

Or is that me? It's all getting jumbled up. I hear someone hiss 'Alex!' in a harsh voice and I say, 'No, I'm not Alex. I'm Cal. I'm Cal . . . I'm not Alex. I'm not a lab rat. I'm Cal Conway.'

I'm me.

Eventually the van comes to a stop. The doors open and daylight scorches my eyes.

I'm dragged out and thrown roughly onto a metal trolley.

An ugly grey building comes into sight. This isn't the Facility . . . it's . . . Riley Hall?

What? It can't be . . . can it? I twist my head to try to look properly but this makes everything spin sickeningly fast. I groan and lift a hand to my forehead. I'm burning up inside, but my skin feels icy cold and clammy against my fingers. I'm shivery all over and my teeth chatter. Faces loom in and out at me and I hear someone say, 'Tell Cavendish he'll have to delay things. He's in no fit state,' and then there's only darkness.

I wake up in what looks like a hospital room. My arm is hooked up to a bag of liquid. My head throbs with a rhythm like someone is banging a stick against it. The memory of being captured comes at me like a freight train and I groan, running my tongue over cracked, dry lips.

The door opens and Daniel Cavendish comes in with another man. 'Hello, Cal,' Cavendish says. 'Are you feeling better? You had a very severe infection in that hand.'

I try to turn my head to look around. An image of being taken into a big grey building comes into my mind.

'Where am I?' I say croakily. 'Is this Riley Hall?'

Cavendish frowns. 'The Facility was built in the old prison known as Riley Hall. They're one and the same place. The Securitat is very keen for our research to correct offenders' behaviour.'

Of course. I never saw the building when Torch rescued me. I left in the dark.

I was in Riley Hall all that time.

I wince at the bright light and squeeze my eyes closed again, trying to take this in. Riley Hall, the Facility, me, the boy Alex . . . it's like a series of circles all rippling closer together. My life and his, mixed up in a way that can never be separated. All squeezing into something small and tight, like a noose around my neck.

'I know what you did,' I say. 'You pretended I was dead and brought me here for your research. And the donor boy . . . he was a prisoner here, wasn't he?'

Cavendish purses his lips. 'Alex Hunt was the first young offender to be part of our programme of research here, yes.'

'What do you want from me?' My lips are so dry they stick to my teeth. 'Why won't you leave me alone?'

'All our research rests on you. We have to take things up a notch. Move to the next level.'

I try to struggle upwards and then realise I'm bound by my wrists to the bed. 'What are you going to do to me?'

'We're simply putting you back into the world you know so well, that's all. You're perfectly safe. Didn't we keep you alive these past twelve years? We didn't hurt you.'

'What?' I struggle against the bindings again but they

get tighter. 'You stole my life!' I yell. 'You had no right! And what about Alex? You killed him, didn't you? For your stupid experiment.'

Cavendish looks uncomfortable. 'Nothing inhumane was done here to anyone. There are sometimes unfortunate and unexpected consequences, that's all.'

'You're disgusting,' I whisper. 'The whole programme is disgusting! And I won't be part of it again! I won't let you do it!' I thrash about wildly, shaking my head and pulling against the restraints.

Cavendish sighs. 'We can easily sedate you, so it's pointless behaving that way. You'll only injure yourself. But I'd prefer it if you were a willing patient, especially as you may endanger my staff who are trying to treat you. Maybe I should show you something . . .' He produces a phone from his pocket. He points it at the wall and a projection comes to life. It's a prison cell in semi-darkness. The image pans around the room. I see Jax, lying on the hard bench, his big trainers hanging off the end. It's so realistic, I get an urge to touch him. Tell him it's OK.

But it isn't. None of it's OK. It may never be OK again.

He's got Jax. But not Kyla? Maybe she got away. And it looks like my mother got away too. I guess they didn't know who she was. I hold this comforting thought inside, cherishing it. Holding it close. But poor Jax . . . What will they do to him? Will he be next for the Revealer Chip?

'I'll do anything you want,' I say flatly. 'Just let him go.' I don't know if I can trust Cavendish, but it's all I have to hang on to – the thought that my friend won't get hurt.

'Good, I'm glad you're seeing sense,' says Cavendish crisply. 'Now those antibiotics have brought you back round to us, we can begin the procedure.' He smiles but there's no humour in his eyes. 'You could think of it as going home.'

I turn my head to the wall. I'm numb and cold inside. Nothing could be worse than this. I almost wish I'd never woken up in the first place. Never had a taste of a real life. Of friendship. Maybe even love.

It's over. I'm going back. Back into the coma world.

CHAPTER 29

a perfect smile

I don't struggle or resist. How could I? Jax's life might depend on my cooperation. They attach me to tubes with needles under my skin. I'm in the bed for now and I wonder if they'll put me in the pod later, once I'm out? I glance across the room at it and lick my dry lips. They'll put me in and keep me there, like a spider under a glass.

I keep my eyes wide open as long as I can but it's no use.

I don't fall down a hole or go towards a light or anything like that.

Everything just sort of shifts.

One minute I'm in a bed in Riley Hall, the next, I'm standing in the middle of the school playground. People are playing football around me and it's like the world is spinning and loud and I'm the only thing still and quiet. I look around and everything feels one hundred per cent real. The ball comes towards me and I instinctively block it and cross it back to the nearest boy. It felt like a real ball and the boy who mumbles 'Cheers' is as solid as I am. I take a deep sniff and that's how I can tell the difference. It doesn't smell like anything at all here. I lift my arm and smell my own armpit. Nothing. Like I'm just some sort of 3D avatar.

The whistle goes for the end of breaktime but I just walk towards the gates. I hear an adult voice shout at me but don't bother to turn round. I can do what I like. Outside the school I cross the road and don't bother looking. I feel the whoosh of cars going past but of course, nothing hits me. You'd think that would be liberating but it isn't. I feel numb inside.

A thought hits me forcefully then. I suddenly know with more certainty than I've ever felt that Cavendish won't free my friend. And they'll probably kill me if I ever wake up again. There's nothing to lose. This is my chance to wreck things for the Facility, even if I die in the attempt.

I start to walk in the familiar direction. There's no one around at all. Now I've made up my mind, my brain has stopped bothering to people this movie with extras. I lift a single finger into the sky and shout, 'Are you getting all this, Cavendish?' Something moves at the corner of my eye and I flinch but it's only that cat again. I feel a tug of affection and squat down, coaxing it over. The cat arches its back, rubbing against my legs.

'You can't help being owned by an ugly, bald creep, can you, puss?' I look at the cat again and this time I notice its collar. I undo the little leather pouch. The small black tracker is in there. It seems small, considering the damage it did when it was cut out.

I hold it up to the sky and shout again, telling Cavendish exactly where he can shove his tracker. I'm quite enjoying swearing at the sky like a madman. No men in white coats can come and get me, can they? The men in white coats already came.

As I get closer, I can feel my feet getting heavy, just like in a dream, but I force myself into a run and even though it takes twice as long as it should, I finally get to the top of the hill.

I go to the pile of bricks at the side of the house. I take aim and throw one straight through the window. It makes a satisfying sound, just like a real window breaking.

The front door hangs open and an eerie wind whistles through the rooms. Inside, it's derelict now and broken glass and dirt crunches underfoot.

I'm going to fight Cavendish with everything I've got – trash his research and stop the nightmare he's planning. It ends here. With me. I'm going to smash up this fake world.

I go outside to the shed and throw open the door. I know there's an axe in here somewhere.

The wind is whipping up now, buffeting against the metal walls. A high-pitched sound like distant screaming curls around me.

I see the axe resting up against the broken work bench and heft it onto my shoulder. A shadow passes across the open doorway, fast, like an animal. My mouth goes dry and my heart starts to hammer.

'It's not real . . . none of it is real.' I whisper the words quietly to myself but they don't really help. It *feels* real, is the thing. The hairs on the back of my neck are standing up for real and the wind is blowing in my face for real as I move towards the door, which suddenly slams shut. I stumble forward, trying to not fall on the axe, and I reach for the door . . . and then I hear quiet laughter behind me. All the terror of being shut in here all those times hits me like a tsunami and I fight down the urge to scream and shout. I make myself close my eyes and keep my back turned, even though I hear heavy breathing and the warmth of another, bigger body behind me. I have no reason to be scared. But I can't make it go away. Not like I could with everything else.

That's when I realise what's really happening . . .

Cavendish talked about the next phase of this project, didn't he? He isn't just watching any more – he's found a way to get inside and manipulate my thoughts. He's been rummaging around inside my head and looking for my weaknesses. He knows what buttons to press. He knows my fears and how to exploit them to his own advantage.

What better way to keep people down than planting scary images in their heads? Nowhere is safe. No *one* is safe. That's what they want everyone to think. They can mess with people's minds and scare them into submission.

No. I can't let them get away with it. 'You can't hurt me, Cavendish!' I shout. 'This Des isn't real. He's just a bad dream. *You* don't even scare me.' The last part isn't true. I feel hot breath against the back of my neck and a rough hand grabs a handful of my hair. It's all I can do not to cry out or turn round. 'You're nothing,' I say. 'No one. You're not even real. You're nothing.'

I'm a millisecond away from freaking out and fighting back but I know if I do, I'll be lost. I'll have allowed myself to become part of this world again, just by accepting it's real. My heart is racing, I'm sweating all over . . . Got to hold out a bit longer. I can feel myself slipping. I've got to turn round! Got to fight him off! If I can just hang on a bit longer. I close my eyes and say, 'No, no, no, no, no.'

The door slams open again and I know I'm alone. I laugh out loud, euphoric at having beaten him.

I run out into the light. There isn't much of it left because the sky is bunched with black clouds and thunder is rumbling away. It feels like a massive storm is brewing. The air tastes metallic. I'm sweating all over as I go back into the house, the heavy axe on my shoulder. Outside Pigface's room I swing it back and bring it hard into the door with a crunch. It melts away like it was never there. I walk over to the broken Xbox, which is sitting just where I last saw it on the cabinet, split across the top. It's been repaired. No damage from where the weights fell on it. It looks different in other ways too. There's no Microsoft or Xbox logo. It's just a black box, with a whole load of tiny lights on it, flashing away. I've seen it before, back in the room where my real body is lying like a corpse on a slab.

Realisation slams into me. This is the brain of the Cracks programme.

Everything that happened to Alex in his real life got

mixed up with what was happening to me as I hung, trapped inside that pod. The nurse mum. The cat.

The Xbox.

He broke Ryan's Xbox and it set off a chain of events that ended up with him inside Riley Hall, a prisoner. His memories and my imagination combined and created a whole new reality.

The Xbox, the Cracks hard disk . . . they've somehow come together in my mind. I might not be able to touch it in this world, but maybe I can take away its power.

All I know is, my mind is my own now. I won't be controlled by a lump of plastic, even a lump of plastic that can communicate with a chip inside my brain.

I look at the axe in my hand and there's a moment's hesitation. Will it hurt me to this? Will it set me free?

But then I realise that I don't even care. If I have to die, I'll die on *my* terms. In control.

I lift the axe up, ready to crack the box in two and then freeze. A strange sound fills the room. It's a girl, crying, somewhere outside. It sounds like someone is hurting her.

'Cal! Cal! Help me, please help me!'

It's Kyla's voice.

She's not real, she's not real.

Wait. What if this is the real Kyla? What if my ears are hearing what's actually happening around me in the Facility? My insides clench with fear. 'Kyla!' I call out. 'Where are you?' I turn around blindly and stagger into the hallway, trying to see where she is, but the wind is so strong I can hardly stand up, even though I'm inside.

I realise then that the crying's coming from 'my' bedroom. I push open the door and step inside.

The storm instantly stops, like someone switched it off. Instead, the sun is slanting through the window onto her face. She's sleeping, one hand curled up under her chin. She's wearing some sort of short blue dress and her long brown legs seem to gleam. She's smiling in her sleep and then she rolls onto her back and stretches sleepily, stretching her toes so her dress rides up a little further up her thighs.

She opens her eyes. 'Cal,' she says dreamily. 'I've missed you. Come here.' She holds her arms out to me.

It feels like a giant magnet is pulling me towards her. I can't stop myself. I don't care if it's not real. I could be with her, here, for ever. She wants me. She actually wants me. Heart banging and palms sweating, I sit down on the edge of the bed and start to lean over. Her lips are slightly parted and she gives a little sigh as I get closer. My lips are just about to touch hers when I notice it. The gap between her teeth has gone.

I jump back like someone has hit me.

This isn't Kyla.

Her eyes snap open. 'What's the matter, Cal?' she says. She's smiling like I'm the most desirable thing she's ever seen. Then I see that the teeth aren't the only thing wrong. She uncurls her fingers to reach for me and I notice her hands. Instead of bitten nails with chipped varnish, she has perfect, long fingernails tipped with snow-white crescents. It's all wrong. These aren't Kyla's hands. She's too perfect now.

No, she's the wrong kind of perfect.

I stand up, shakily. He's somehow been in my mind while I was recovering, used that Revealer Chip and seen how I feel about her and he's using it against me. For a second, I burn all over with embarrassment and have to squeeze my fists tight. I close my eyes and swallow. What else did he see? Those thoughts are mine. They're no one else's. They're not even for Kyla.

A kind of white rage fills me up like light inside then and I know I can do this. 'Forget it,' I say, turning to leave. 'This isn't going to work.' I don't see her move, but Kyla is suddenly right there, blocking the door now. Her eyes are half closed and sexy and she reaches for the zip of my hoodie and starts to pull on it.

'Stay with me, Cal,' she says. 'Believe in me. We can be together always here. You know you want to. Just one kiss, come on . . .'

My body seems to have a life of its own because I feel myself melting towards her. What's the harm? It's just one kiss . . .

Then I picture the real Kyla, and Jax, who's curled up in a prison cell. Does he have her too? Will he hurt them, like he's hurt me? I force myself to shove the pretend Kyla out of the way. She screams and falls back, hard, and it takes everything I've got to wrench the door open.

I take one last look back. Her eyes are burning into me.

'Come on, Cal . . . what's stopping you?' she says, but she sounds weird. And then I realise; it's not Kyla's lovely voice I'm hearing. It's Cavendish's voice.

All the hairs on the back of my neck go up. But it's not going to work. Cavendish is just trying to scare me. He's set traps for me here in this coma world, knowing I'll fight back. And I won't let him win.

I run back to where I left the axe. I pick it up and start smashing it into the walls of the hallway.

Huge cracks appear along the walls and start to spread quickly. The ground starts to rumble under my feet like an earthquake. Plaster and dust patter onto my face and catch in my throat just like it's real. But the world has gone red and the rumbling turns into the sound of a heartbeat, loud and rhythmic, all around me.

I smash down the door to Ryan's room and lift the axe over the black box. As the blade smashes down into the hard plastic, the world explodes around me and blinding light fills the room.

This is it, it's the end.

A sharp pain slices into my head and I crouch down, instinctively trying to protect myself. The world goes still and I look up, wincing at the brightness.

I'm in a perfectly white room, with no chairs or tables. I know somehow that I have to get out or I'll die here. I run full pelt at a window. I hear it break but it feels like something molten and I'm pushing against it, fighting it.

I shout, 'NO!' at the top of my voice, over and over again. My voice has gone all slow and drawly. I hear an almighty cracking sound.

Chapter 30

pilot lights

For a minute I think I'm trapped inside a gigantic spider web. I can feel it everywhere, sticky and tangled around me. Then I realise I'm back in the real world, inside the pod. I kick and thrash about and suddenly I'm free, slumping sideways against the moist glass surface.

I find the pod door and climb out, wincing at the worst headache of my life. The light of the room is pure violence but right at that moment there's a weird *fpzzt* sound and the room goes dark.

I feel a shudder of pure panic. Am I still in the coma? Did I make that happen? But no, I can smell things . . . bleach, disinfectant . . . smoke. It's real. I really am back!

All of a sudden, lights come on again, but much dimmer and they keep flickering. Back-up lights, maybe. It hits me that no one seems to be watching me or they would have come in by now. Why? This unnerves me more than almost anything else. I look around for my clothes and can't see them anywhere, then spot a trolley over by the door. It looks like the laundry one I escaped in before but when I open it, I see that it contains rubbish: old tissues, plastic cups and paper towels. Then I spot something that chills me to the bone. The toe of one of my trainers is just visible, poking up from beneath a big wad of paper towels. I gingerly reach inside and find it and its partner. My clothes are rolled into a ball underneath.

It takes a second to make sense of the true horror of this.

They were throwing away my clothes. Throwing them away because I wasn't ever coming back. There's a white overall in the bin too, made of some incredibly light material. I've seen some of the guards wearing them. It has a hood with a see-through mask at the front.

Shaking hard, I pull everything on, including the overall. I do up my laces with fumbling, sausage fingers. I step out into the corridor and listen. It's eerily quiet.

Got to find Jax and Kyla and get the hell out of here. Cavendish said the Facility was built onto Riley Hall. I suddenly remember the old burned out wing that Loz and Alex must have helped clean out. I wonder if that's where they built the new wing? Got to get my bearings and find some sort of map.

Someone comes around the corner then, a guard, dressed like me, and my heart seems to stop.

'Why are you still here?' says the man. 'They're locking down this whole area. Has the boy been moved yet?'

'Yes, he's just gone. I'm on my way,' I say in a gruff voice. Thank God he's distracted, speaking into his phone and he carries on, barking orders to someone else.

It's clear I can't just wander about. I go back into the room again, thinking hard.

I remember the cells were in rows above the large central area. I just have to trust that this memory from the coma world is accurate. Another memory comes to me . . . and I look up.

This room has the same square ventilation shaft I saw in the kitchens.

Maybe they run round the whole building.

I pat my pockets, dearly wishing I still had my lock picks. But they're gone.

Then something occurs to me. I put my hand into the trolley bin and reach down, rooting around for ages. I'm on the verge of giving up when my fingers close around something metal that jangles . . .

Brilliant! I give the lock picks a little kiss.

I quickly work out how to make the bed as high as it will go and then climb on. Using the picks, I undo the ventilation covering and hoist myself inside. I'm weak from the infection and coma and it's not easy. I'm sweating as I try for the third time and manage to get my belly over the ledge. Then I slide inside and replace the covering.

It's warm in here and dust hangs in huge ropes all around. I try not to think about spiders. I don't know which direction I'm going but decide that if I can find the big open area in the old prison, I can find where the cells are and look for Jax.

I start shuffling forwards. It's hard work. My knees and back are soon aching and the hot dusty air is making me wheeze. I'm sweating all over. After finding myself up against a few dead ends, my luck changes. The shaft gets big enough to walk with my head down. Plus I can see that I'm finally in the old bit of the building. Through the vents, I glimpse grey stone floor below and a smell of dampness, sweat and age.

Shouts draw me on faster and suddenly I'm looking down on the central atrium of Riley Hall, the one where the boy jeered at me that time. I give my head a shake. That didn't happen to me. It happened to the donor boy.

Something weird is going on below. A handful of teenage boy prisoners are smashing stuff up, throwing tables and chairs about and cat-calling triumphantly. A siren goes off – *wah-wah-wah* – and guards suddenly spill into the area. Tasers go off in a blinding flash. The prisoners are over-powered within seconds, pathetically easily. The guards start hauling the prisoners away, yelling about getting out of the building.

In no time it becomes unnaturally quiet. I crawl to the nearest vent covering, which is over one of the long balconies. Like the others though, the screws are on the other side. I have to kick it repeatedly until it buckles and then finally falls with a crash to the ground. The sound is horribly loud.

I peer down. It looks like a long way to the balcony.

I lower myself onto my belly backwards and hold on to the rim as long as possible before jumping.

Three, two, one . . .

I jump. My ankle twists a bit but I'm OK. I start to walk along the balcony. All the cell doors are open. Jax has probably already been taken to wherever the other prisoners are going. But I have to be sure. I've got to get him away from Cavendish.

I carefully look inside each cell, one by one. Many of them have had the bunk beds wrenched from the wall and there are dark stains on the wall. Looks like there was some sort of riot here. I walk the full length of two balconies but don't see a single prisoner.

Maybe I should just get out of here.

But wait . . . what was that? I stand utterly still, listening, and then hear it again. A low moaning coming from the very first room I looked into. I run in and then notice something I didn't see before: a brown hand poking out from behind the broken bed.

'Jax? Is that you?' It takes ages to heave the bunk bed to one side but eventually it shifts. Jax is lying behind it, a big gash on his head and his arm lying at an odd angle.

'Jax!'

His eyelids flutter and then he's looking at me. Some cloud of confusion passes over his face and then recognition flares in his eyes, like tiny pilot lights being switched on.

'Matt!' he says hoarsely. 'Or whatever your bloody name is!' He says it like we've just bumped into each other in the street and even tries to lift his arm to touch knuckles. But pain makes him gasp.

'I'm going to get you out of here,' I say. 'Where's Kyla?'

'They didn't get her,' he says with an effort. 'We had a

bit of an argument and she'd stomped off. Then they got me.'

A tiny part of my brain wants to know what they were arguing about despite everything going on right now. But I'm so relieved she got away. It proves what I guessed before, that Cavendish looked at my thoughts – and hopes – and then used them against me.'Let's get you up,' I say.

It hurts him. A lot. I help him get to his feet, his teeth bared against the pain. I can see that his arm is giving him agony. I'm still so happy to see him that I have to blink a few times and rub my sleeve across my face. Jax smiles back at me.

'You saved me, man,' he says, his voice still rough. He coughs and groans. 'I don't know what's going on. The lads I shared with went nuts and they didn't even care that I was hurt.'

'Well, let's get out of here,' I say. 'We're heading for the kitchens. There's an exit there.'

'How'd you know?' says Jax. 'And why are you even *here*?'

'It's a long story, mate,' I say. 'It'll have to wait, come on.'

The siren is still going off at ear-splitting volume. I try to remember which way to go and think I've got it when we turn a corner and a figure in black with a balaclava covering their face springs out, pointing the barrel of a gun directly at us.

Then I hear a sharp intake of breath. The masked person reaches up and pulls off the balaclava.

'*Tom?*' For a second I think I must be dreaming or

doing his best, but his injuries slow him down. Tom yells back at us to hurry and we put on a burst of speed that makes Jax shudder with agony. We turn corners and skid on broken glass as we rush to the kitchen door. We feel the rumbles of the first bomb going off through our feet and know we have seconds until they go off in turn. Part of me wants to let go of Jax and save my own skin but I force myself to hold on to his good arm tightly, not trusting myself to let him go. We run through the kitchen and out to the storeroom where the door leads outside. We scramble to open it, and there's a shuddering blast behind us that knocks all of us off our feet.

And then we're outside. There's a strange moment of quiet, a gap in time where I feel fresh air on my face. Tom's yelling but I can't hear. His mouth is stretched wide. I throw myself forwards as an explosion rips the world apart.

I can taste and smell burned hair as I tumble onto the hard ground with a crunch and roll over. A wall of heat follows me. I stagger to my feet, unable to see anything but black, choking smoke. I run and throw myself onto grass, my lungs tearing apart as I try to pull air into them. Tom is next to me, coughing violently. I look up at the building that's smoking and crumbling and cracking with the roar of flames.

The thought just seems to float down into my mind like the bits of charred stuff that are raining down on me.

Jax.

Where's Jax?

I scramble to my feet and then see him, lying face down

about three metres away. I run over and turn him over onto his back, forgetting to be careful with his broken arm. He has an ugly gash on his forehead but his brown eyes are open, looking up at me.

He's OK!

I shake him. 'Jax! Jax, come on! Move! Come on, man, you're going to be all right!' I shake him harder but he won't respond and his head just lolls to the side.

I cradle him and cry angry gulping sobs. 'Come on!'

Why won't he move? Why wasn't he faster? Why did he have to break an arm? Why was he even here?

And then Tom is trying to pull me away and saying, 'Come away, Cal. You can't do anything now, come away.' It's only then that I look properly at his eyes.

The little pilot lights I saw before . . . they've gone out.

Chapter 31

it's really you

Snot, blood, tears and dirt are smeared all over my face and I can't stop coughing. I can't seem to let go of Jax, like my arms are locked round his neck. All I can think is, 'How am I going to tell Kyla?' and 'It's my fault.'

I only realise I'm rocking when something makes me stop and I look up to see Nathan there. I don't know where he came from but he's here. He's squatting on his haunches and taking hold of my arms, gently prising them away from Jax's body. He doesn't seem so angry now. He looks sad and kind.

'Come on, buddy,' he says softly. 'There's nothing you can do for him. We have to get out of here quickly. Come on.' He's speaking gently but his grip is strong and I find myself being lifted to my feet.

'We have to take him!' I shout and then bend double into a fit of coughing.

There are sirens in the distance but I don't care. I'm going to stay here with Jax.

Tom and another man lift Jax up, carefully but quickly. Nathan pulls me to my feet and steers me fast to a van with blacked out windows. I'm just about to get in when I look down and see something by my feet. It's the cat.

I reach down and pick up its furry, warm body and pull it close. It's been with me right through this. Shown me where to go and even helped me escape. It hums and purrs like a motor and doesn't seem to mind the tears that are dripping onto its back as I climb into the van.

I lay my throbbing head against the window. Everything is tinted grey.

But it isn't just the glass. The world has gone darker too.

one month later

It didn't take long for Torch to find Kyla and bring her to me. She'd been living rough in an abandoned barn in the countryside outside Sheffield, trying to decide what to do. I gave Tom her number and he rang her, using a special phone to hide his ID and location. She was suspicious of him at first and wouldn't believe who he was until he put me on. My face and lips had gone weirdly numb and I tried to force the words out, to say we would come for her, if she could tell us where she was. But she kept firing questions at me about whether I was OK and where Jax was and I couldn't handle it. I gave the phone back to Tom like it was burning me. He must have arranged for someone to collect her because after we'd got back to a safe house, she came bursting in about half an hour later.

She ran into the room and hugged me, or rather the blanket I had around my shoulders, and I just hung my head. I could smell her lovely cinnamon smell and she tried to lift my chin and look me in the eyes but I couldn't and just turned away, burying myself further into the blanket.

I could hear the low murmur of Tom's voice and Kyla shouted, 'No!' then made a high-pitched keening sound. She fell on the ground in a ball with her arms wrapped around herself and sobbed. But I couldn't go to her. Not when I made it happen. It was only because of me that Jax was in Riley Hall in the first place.

I haven't really spoken to her these last few days. We keep catching each other's eyes and looking away, both too wounded and sore to be in each other's space. I'd prefer it if we were fighting.

But that's not all I feel guilty about.

I feel guilty because my friend's dead and happy surges keep lapping inside me. I can't concentrate on anything. Later today, Tom's bringing my mum and dad here. They made us wait, so the authorities didn't realise we'd made contact. I can't believe I'm really going to meet them. I'm shaky and nervous. What if it's all strange? What if they don't like me? It's been such a long time. There's so much to make up for.

At least I understand what happened now. Twelve years

ago, I was in a car accident. That bit was true. My dad was driving. It wasn't his fault.

I was taken to the hospital. A doctor working on a special research project into brain injury persuaded my parents to let them take me to his new unit, which was carrying out cutting edge procedures. His name was Daniel Cavendish.

Then they were told I'd died on the operating table. They weren't allowed to see the body because there had been too much bruising to the head and it would be upsetting. Wild with grief at losing their only child, they accepted the story and buried an empty casket that was given to them by Cavendish. A man who needed a little human lab rat to perfect his secret work.

I still get shaky when I think about being in that pod, all wired up. I get that scary walls-closing-in feeling again. Tom says it'll take a while to get over what they did to me. I wonder if I ever will.

The regime's explanation of the bombing of Riley Hall was that terrorists had smuggled bombs into the building through deliveries to a corrupt guard in the kitchens. They claimed they had a warning in the nick of time and were able to evacuate everyone.

We know different, and other people are catching on too. There have been riots in several cities and Torch say the tide is turning in their favour. No one knows where Cavendish has gone.

I shiver, even though it's not cold.

Then something brings the flicker of a smile to my face. When I was telling Tom about Alex's world, he was very interested in hearing about Des's shed with all his contraband. It may have been a load of old junk he had in there, but some of it, stuff like fertiliser and alarm clocks, can be used in bomb making. And in a regime like this one, that's enough to send CATS round pretty fast. All it took was one anonymous phonecall . . . I bet he made a right fuss when they carted him away. I hope they lock him up for a long time. He shouldn't get away with how he treated Alex.

I lift my face to the warmth of the sunshine. It's peaceful here. The house is owned by Helen Bonaparte's daughter, Sasha, another doctor and her husband Mark, a Torch operative who monitors the news and tells us what's really happening. They're looking after us until we're, as Helen calls it, 'back on our feet'. I was suspicious at first. I felt like I couldn't really trust anyone, not even them. But Helen says they would never have hurt me before. They just wanted to know what they were up against and never would have done anything without my consent. I'm choosing to trust them.

Let's face it, I have to start somewhere. I open my eyes and look across fields that stretch into the distance. It feels as though nothing has really changed for centuries. There are fluffy blobs of sheep here and there and the stone walls make patchwork of the fields.

Something black and white shoots past me and I smile. Sasha named the cat Humphrey. He's in heaven here on the farm, chasing mice and sleeping in the sunshine.

A shape moves into my eye-line by one of the walls.

Squinting into the sunlight, I realise it's Kyla. She lifts her hair up from around her neck and effortlessly twists it into some sort of knot. She dips her head again, wiping hard at her eyes. I'm just about to get up and go back inside again and then I hesitate. I can't avoid her for ever.

I miss her. I miss Jax too. Every time I think about his goofy grin it's like someone knifes me in the chest. I look at the girl sitting on the wall now, her knees drawn into her chest and her arms around them as though she's holding herself in one piece.

Jax has gone but Kyla is still here.

I take a few deep breaths and then walk slowly down the hill towards her. She turns when she hears me and her eyes fill with tears.

Neither of us speaks. I stand there, feeling useless as I always do around her, while she slowly gets to her feet. She wipes her face and our eyes meet.

'Hey you,' I say quietly.

'Hey you, too,' she says and manages a small smile.

'Kyla, I . . .' I feel like someone stole all the words. I'm tongue-tied and feel helpless. But there are really only two words that matter.

'I'm sorry,' I say and gulp as tears blur my vision.

Her eyes go misty and her face crumples. She holds out her arms and we come together like magnets are pulling us close. We just hold each other for ages and ages. It's a long time before she speaks.

'It's not your fault, Matt. Oh, I don't think I can get used to calling you Cal!'

We bend so our foreheads are touching. I've never been this close to her before. Apart from when we slept on that sofa.

'Kyla . . . You're not going to be alone. I'm not going to let you go this time.'

I don't allow myself to think about it. I just tilt my head and kiss her gently on the lips. We stop and then smile at each other. Her eyes sparkle with tears and she looks over my shoulder and then takes a step back from me, giving me a gentle push.

'Later,' she says. 'I think there are some people who want to see you right now.'

I spin round the other way. I can see two middle-aged people: a woman with red hair and a familiar green coat, and a slightly overweight man in jeans and a checked blue shirt. They're both walking quickly up the hill and looking a bit out of breath.

I hear the woman shout. 'Cal?' She clutches the man's arm and runs forward. 'Cal!'

'Go on,' whispers Kyla. 'Hurry!'

I don't need to be told twice.

I start running down the hill.

Acknowledgements

The year 2011 was a big one for me because *Dark Ride* was published, I had to finish *Cracks* and I moved house all within the space of a few months. I owe a massive debt to my editor Anne Clark at Piccadilly Press who was such a calming voice of reason during my many headless chicken impersonations and for her work in helping to shape this story. Huge thanks also to Melissa Hyder for all her excellent suggestions on the text.

I'd like to give profuse and heartfelt thanks to Luisa Plaja, Emily Gale and Alexandra Fouracres for providing immense quantities of support, laughs and virtual tea. My agent Catherine Pellegrino has also provided invaluable support, for which many thanks.

Finally, Pete, Joe and Harry Lownds are owed so much in so many ways that I haven't the space to list them all. I am so lucky to have you guys.

Also by Caroline Green:

A shiver crawled up my spine. It felt like the loneliest place in the world. For a second I thought I caught a snatch of music in the air, but it was just the wind whistling through cracks in the fairground hoardings.
My instincts screamed, 'Run away, Bel! Run away and never return!'
But instead my fingers closed around the ticket in my pocket.
ADMIT ONE.

Bel has never met anyone like Luka. And the day she follows him into the abandoned fairground, she is totally unprepared for the turn her life is about to take . . .

Winner of the RNA Young Adult award
Longlisted for the Branford Boase award

'Full of tension, mystery and real-life drama, Dark Ride is not to be missed.'
Chicklish

'An impressive debut . . . almost impossible to put down.'
Goodreads

S.L. POWELL

Gil is on a collision course with his father,
and when he meets Jude, a passionate activist,
things soon reach crisis point.

As Jude's plans become clear,
Gil is faced with a devastating dilemma
that goes right to the heart of his own identity.

A fast-paced and thought-provoking thriller.

'Riveting story.'
Irish Examiner

'Totally gripping.'
Inkscratchers

*'Gil is a great character and you can really feel his emotions.
You will love this book, especially if you
are into action stories.'*
Bookbabblers